SECRET CODERS

Robots & Repeats

GENE LUEN YANG
& MIKE HOLMES

:01
First Second
New York

"It was this wonderful time between magic and so-called rationality."
—Wally Feurzeig, co-creator of the Logo programming language, on the early days of Logo

First Second
New York

Copyright © 2017 by Humble Comics LLC

Published by First Second
First Second is an imprint of Roaring Brook Press,
a division of Holtzbrinck Publishing Holdings Limited Partnership
175 Fifth Avenue, New York, New York 10010

Library of Congress Control Number: 2016961545

Paperback ISBN: 978-1-62672-605-5
Hardcover ISBN: 978-1-62672-606-2

Our books may be purchased in bulk for promotional, educational,
or business use. Please contact your local bookseller or the Macmillan Corporate
and Premium Sales Department at (800) 221-7945 ext. 5442 or by e-mail at
MacmillanSpecialMarkets@macmillan.com.

First edition 2017

Book design by Rob Steen

Printed in China by Toppan Leefung Printing Ltd., Dongguan City, Guangdong Province

Paperback: 10 9 8 7 6 5 4 3 2 1
Hardcover: 10 9 8 7 6 5 4 3 2 1

Chapter

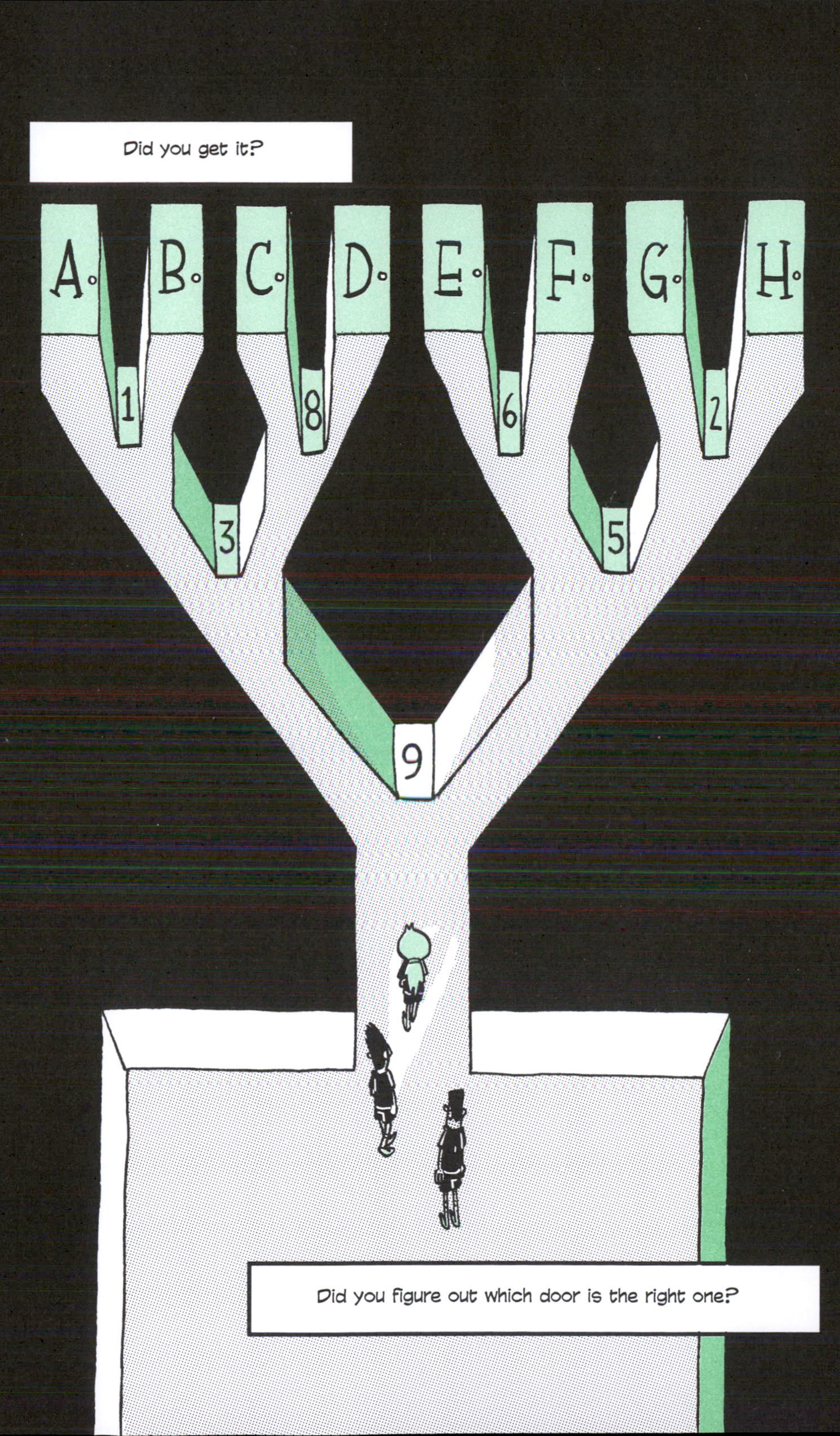
Did you get it?
A.
B.
C.
D.
E.
F.
G.
H.
1
8
6
2
3
5
9
Did you figure out which door is the right one?

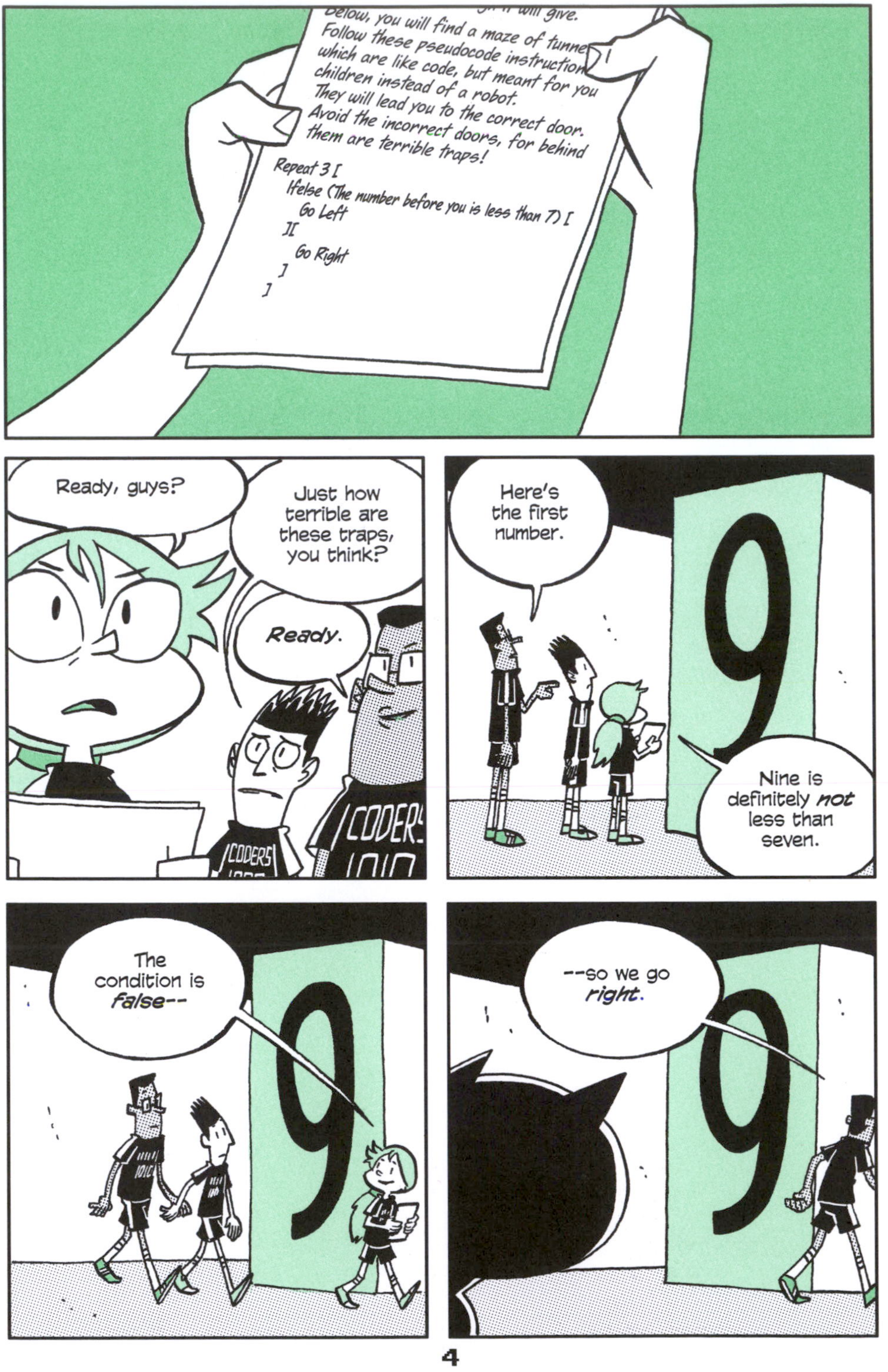
will give.
Below, you will find a maze of tunne
Follow these pseudocode instruction
which are like code, but meant for you
children instead of a robot.
They will lead you to the correct door.
Avoid the incorrect doors, for behind
them are terrible traps!
Repeat 3 [
Ifelse (The number before you is less than 7) [
Go Left
][
Go Right
]
]
Ready, guys?
Just how terrible are these traps, you think?
Ready.
CODERS
Here's the first number.
9
Nine is definitely not less than seven.
The condition is false--
--so we go right.

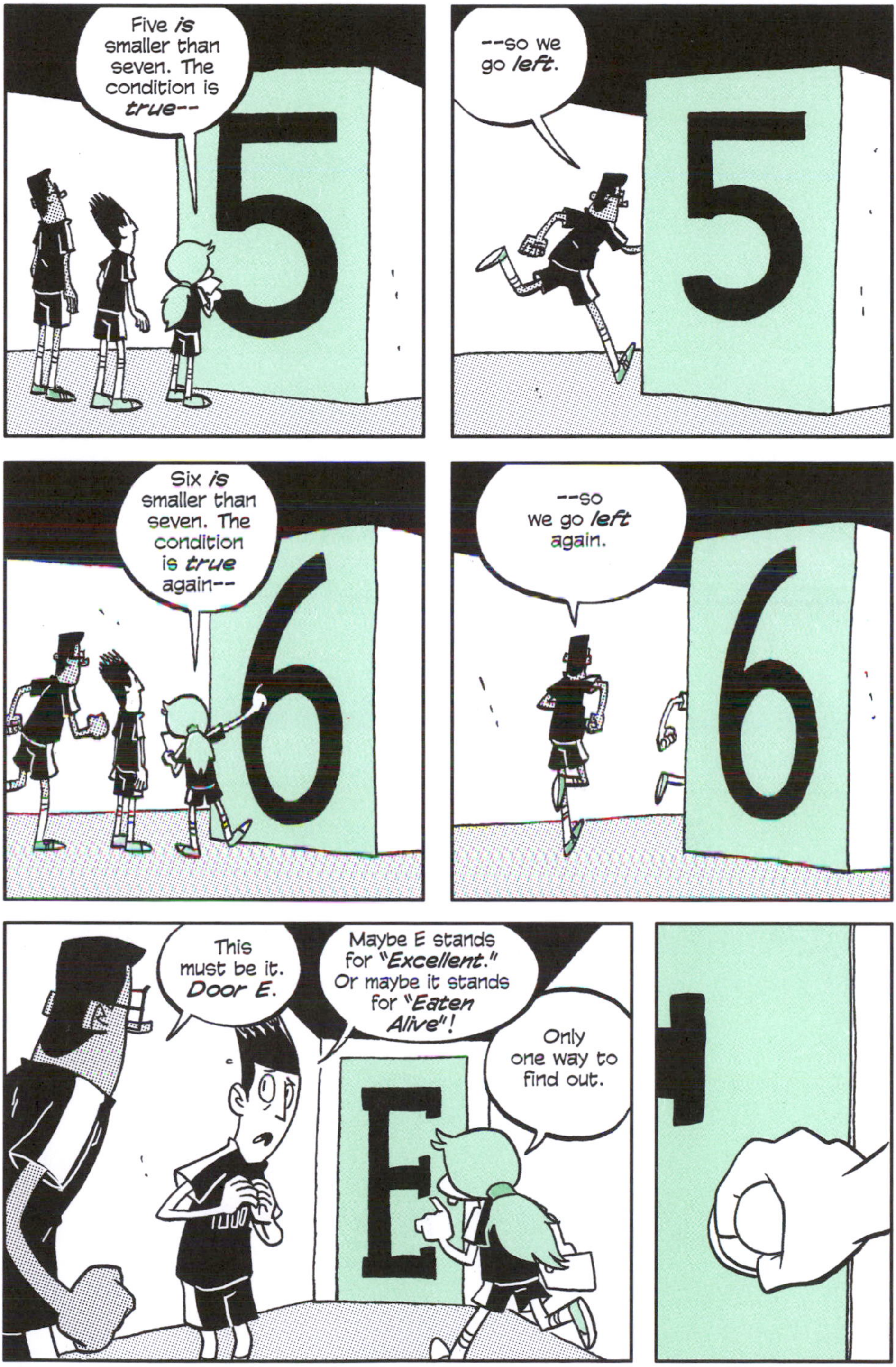

Five *is* smaller than seven. The condition is *true*--
--so we go *left*.
Six *is* smaller than seven. The condition is *true* again--
--so we go *left* again.
This must be it. *Door E*.
Maybe E stands for "*Excellent*." Or maybe it stands for "*Eaten Alive*"!
Only one way to find out.

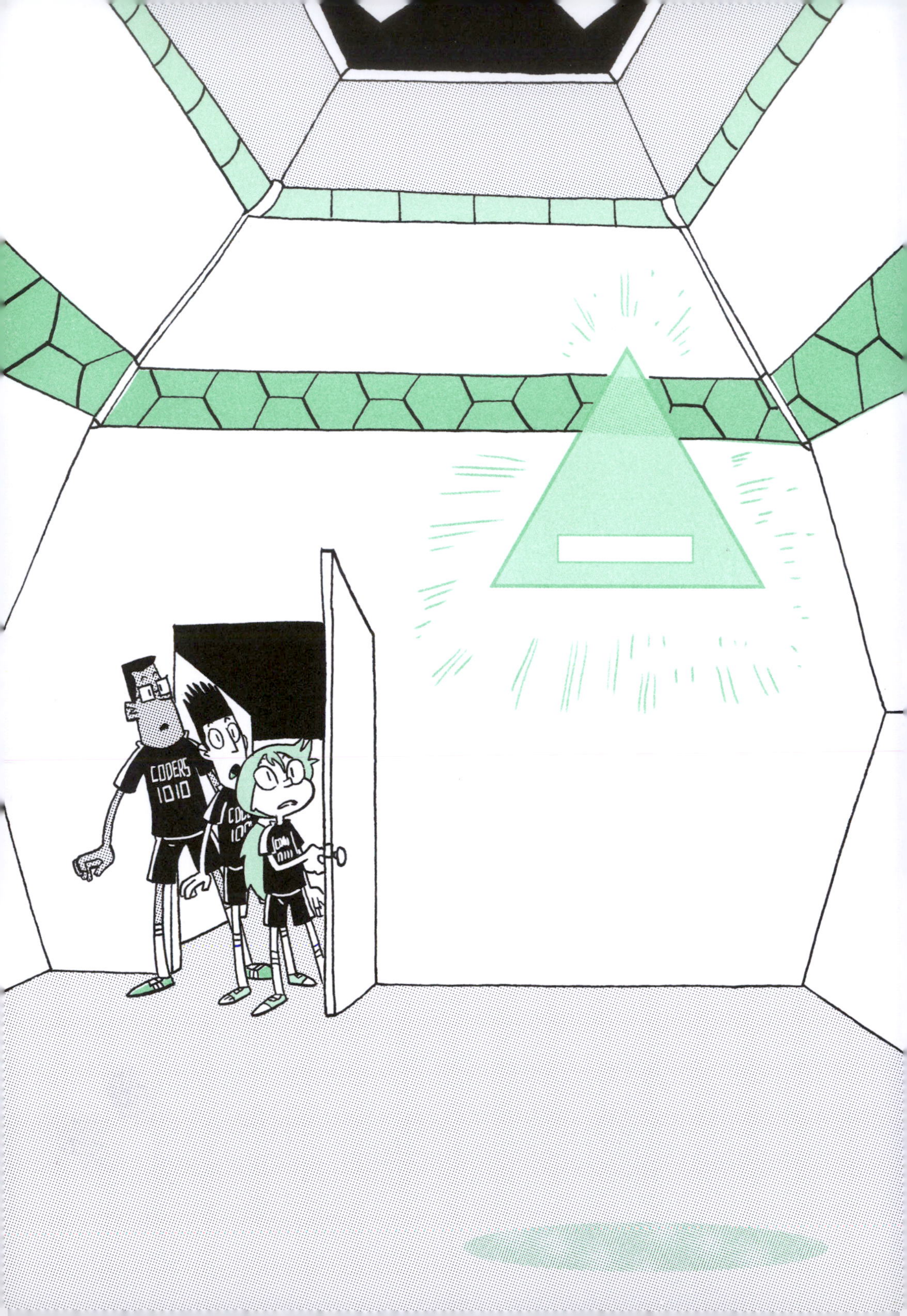
CODERS
1010

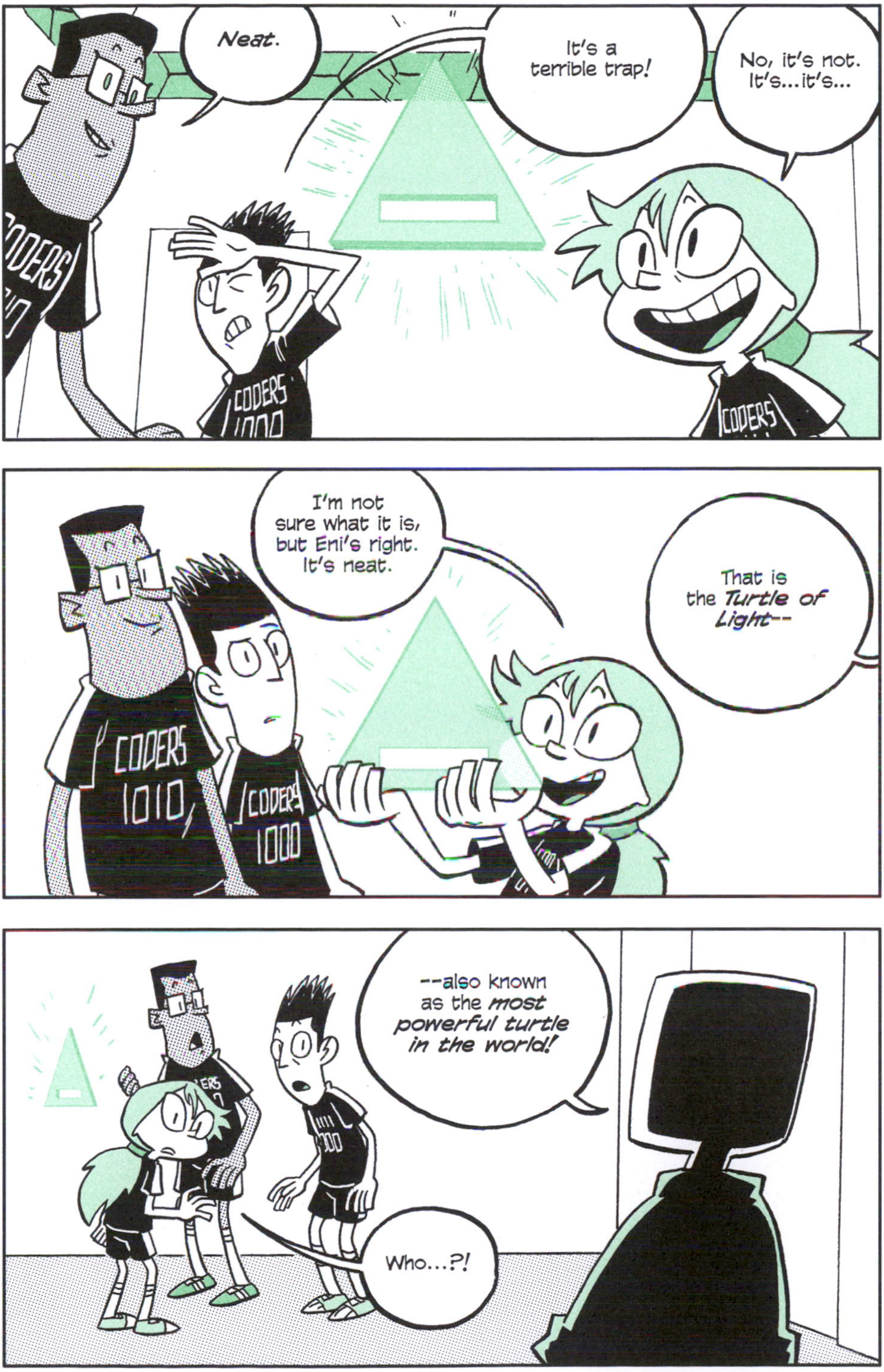
Neat.
It's a terrible trap!
No, it's not. It's...it's...
CODERS 1010
CODERS 1000
CODERS
I'm not sure what it is, but Eni's right. It's neat.
That is the *Turtle of Light*--
CODERS 1010
CODERS 1000
--also known as the *most powerful turtle in the world!*
Who...?!

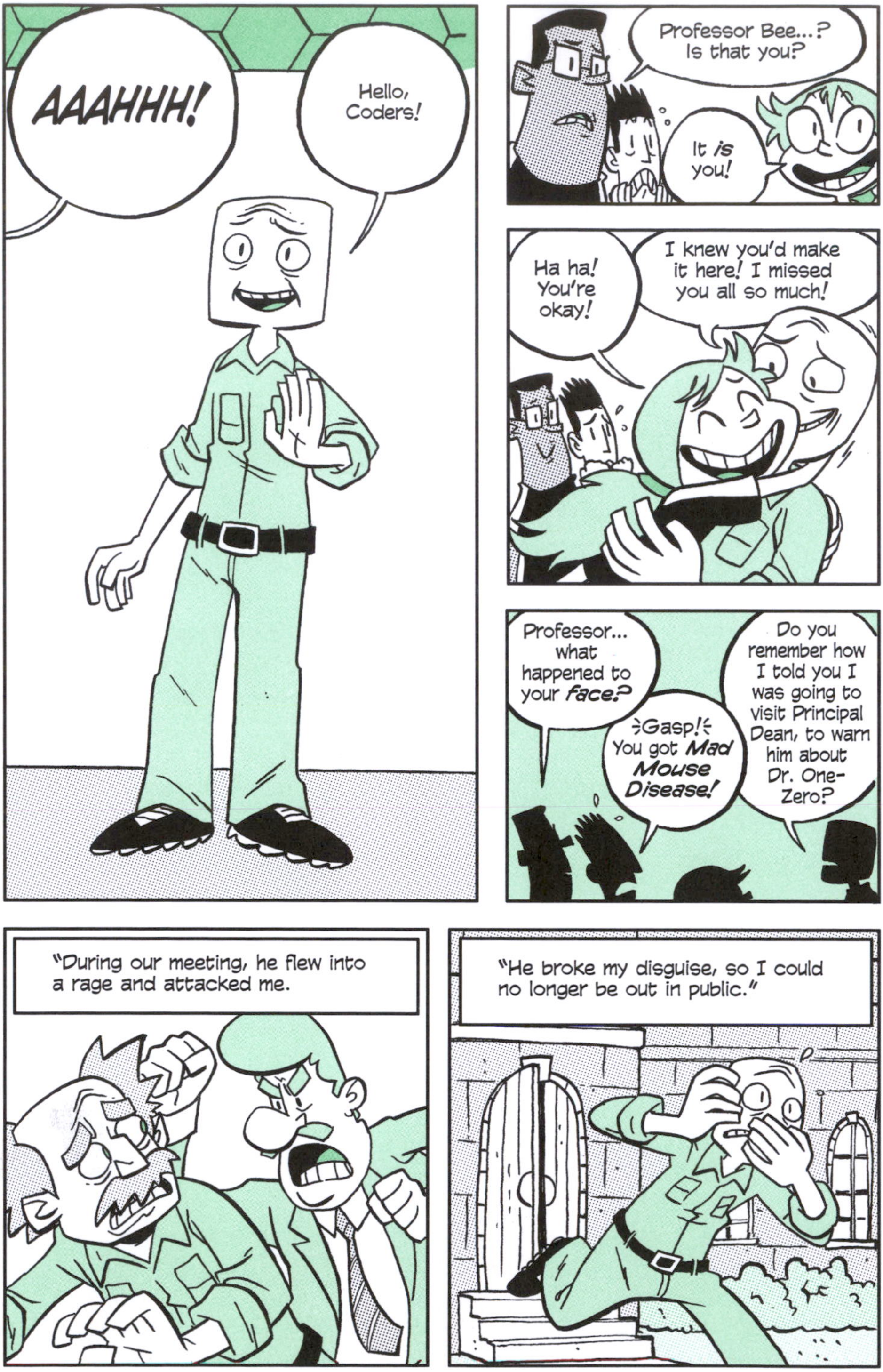
AAAHHH!
Hello, Coders!
Professor Bee...? Is that you?
It *is* you!
Ha ha! You're okay!
I knew you'd make it here! I missed you all so much!
Professor... what happened to your *face?*
Gasp! You got *Mad Mouse Disease!*
Do you remember how I told you I was going to visit Principal Dean, to warn him about Dr. One-Zero?
"During our meeting, he flew into a rage and attacked me.
"He broke my disguise, so I could no longer be out in public."

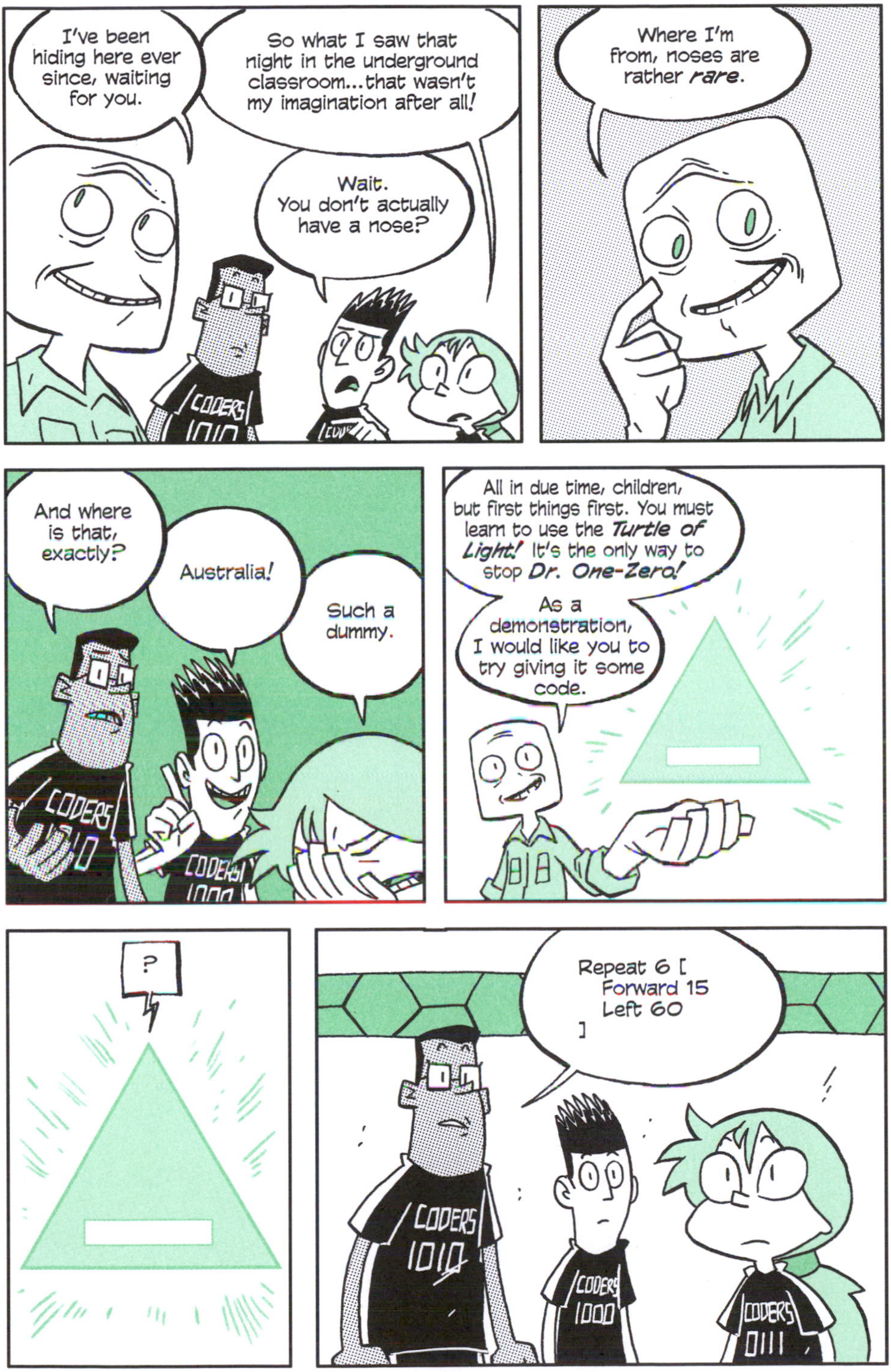
I've been hiding here ever since, waiting for you.
So what I saw that night in the underground classroom...that wasn't my imagination after all!
Wait. You don't actually have a nose?
Where I'm from, noses are rather *rare*.
And where is that, exactly?
Australia!
Such a dummy.
All in due time, children, but first things first. You must learn to use the *Turtle of Light!* It's the only way to stop *Dr. One-Zero!*
As a demonstration, I would like you to try giving it some code.
?
Repeat 6 [
Forward 15
Left 60
]

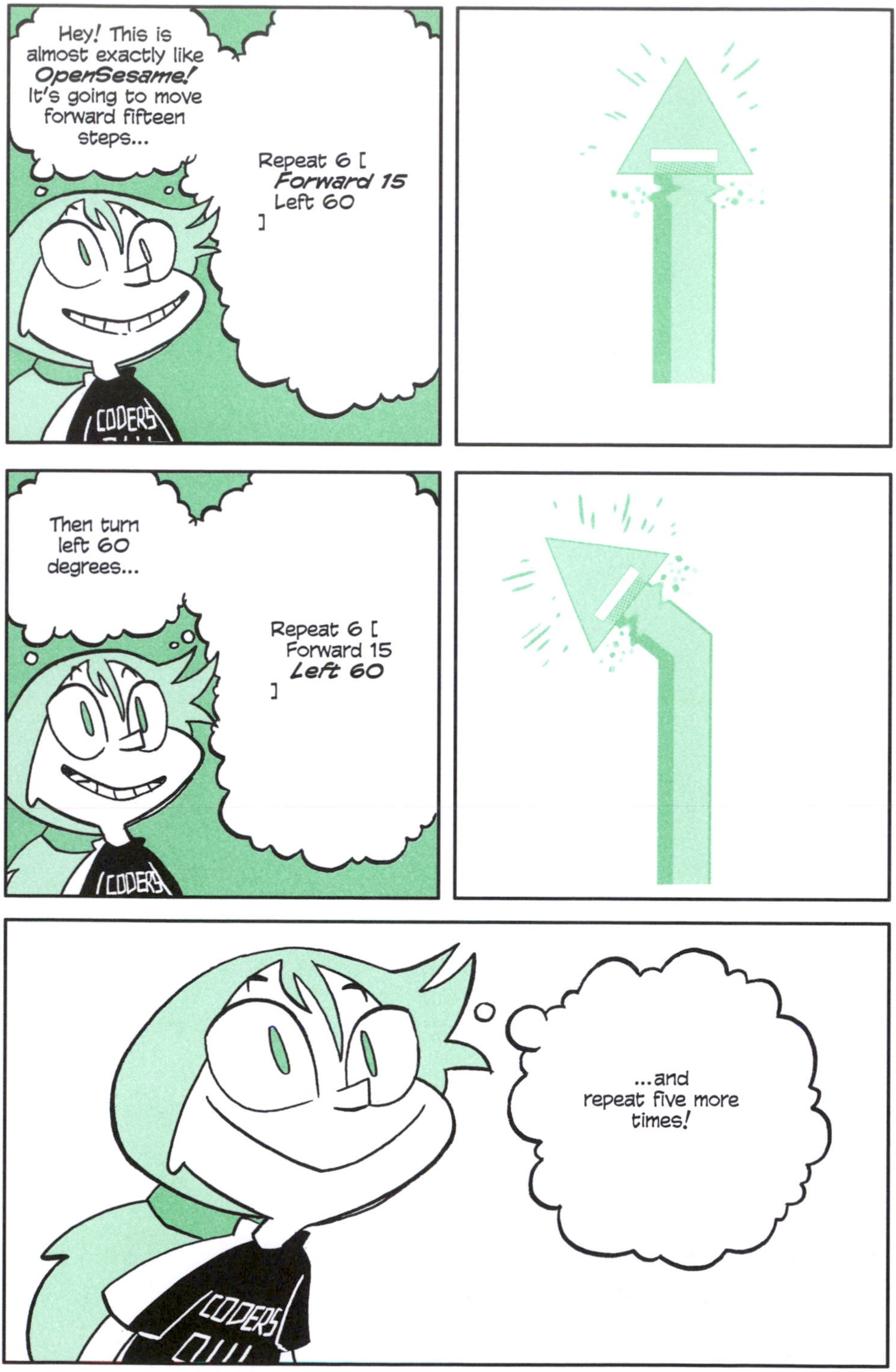

Hey! This is almost exactly like *OpenSesame!* It's going to move forward fifteen steps...
Repeat 6 [
Forward 15
Left 60
]
Then turn left 60 degrees...
Repeat 6 [
Forward 15
Left 60
]
...and repeat five more times!

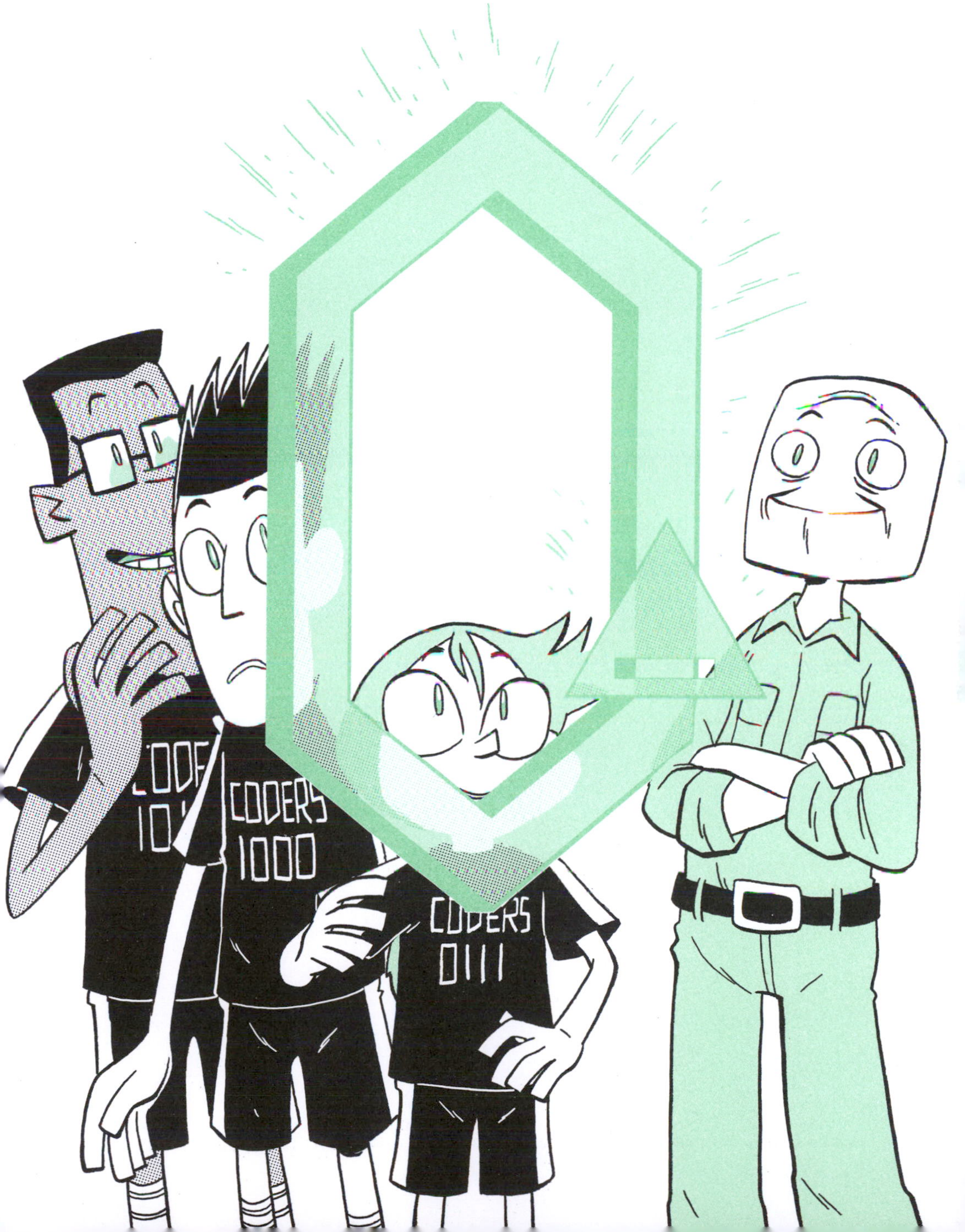
CODERS
1000
CODERS
0111

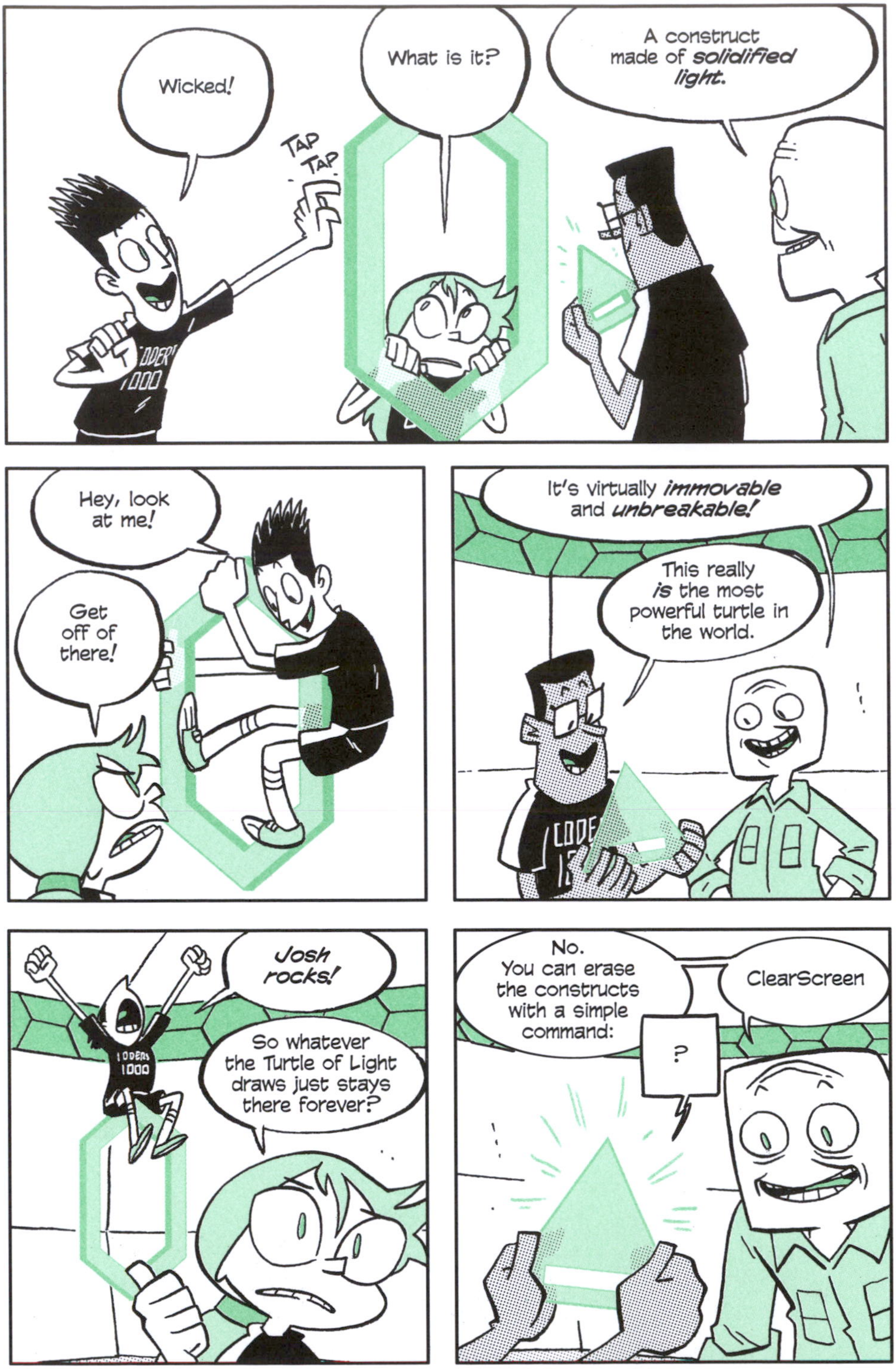

Wicked!
TAP TAP
What is it?
A construct made of *solidified light.*
Hey, look at me!
Get off of there!
It's virtually *immovable* and *unbreakable!*
This really *is* the most powerful turtle in the world.
Josh rocks!
So whatever the Turtle of Light draws just stays there forever?
No. You can erase the constructs with a simple command:
ClearScreen
?

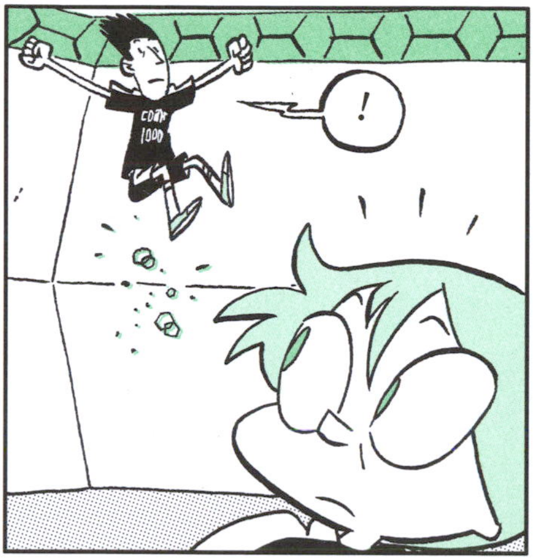
!

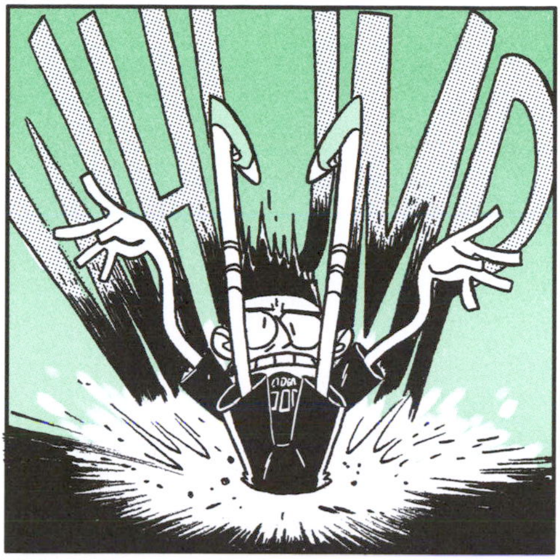

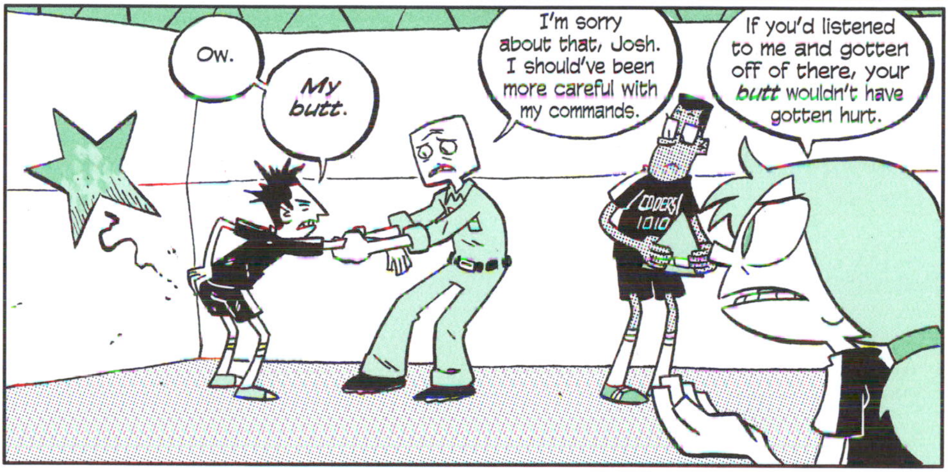
Ow.
My butt.
I'm sorry about that, Josh. I should've been more careful with my commands.
If you'd listened to me and gotten off of there, your butt wouldn't have gotten hurt.

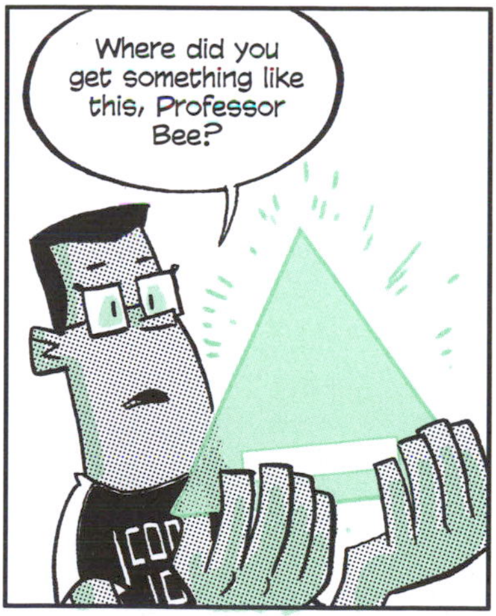
Where did you get something like this, Professor Bee?

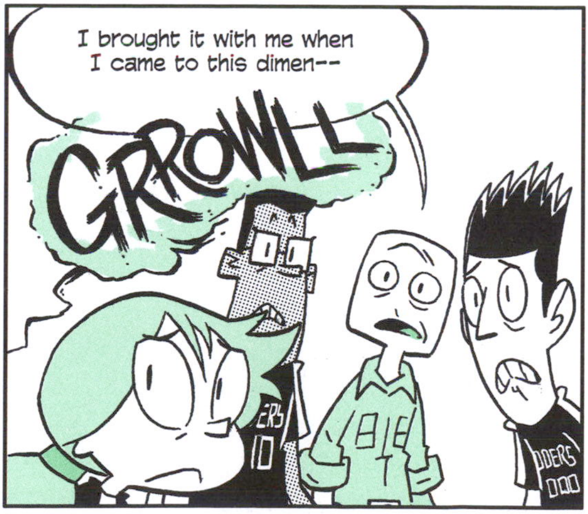
I brought it with me when I came to this dimen--
GRROWLL

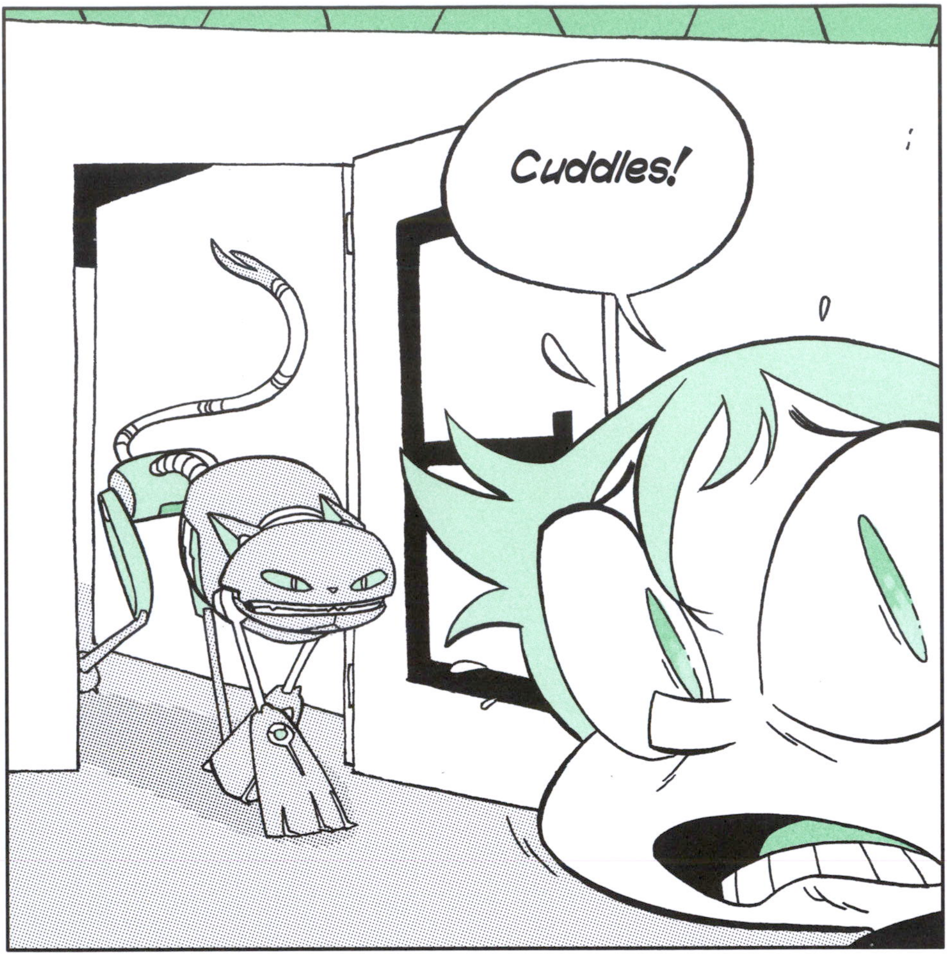
Cuddles!

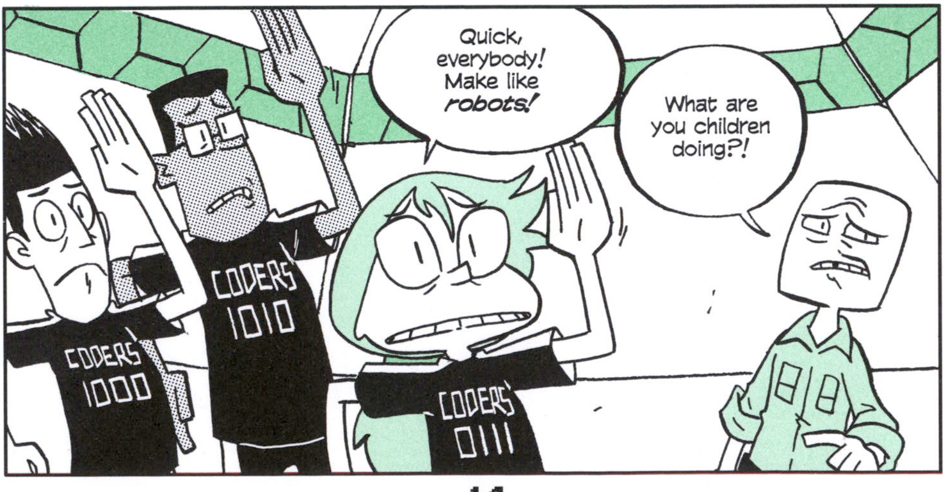
Quick, everybody! Make like *robots!*
What are you children doing?!
CODERS 1000
CODERS 1010
CODERS 0111

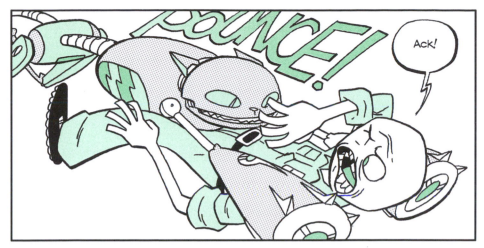

Ack!

Professor Bee!

Stay robotic, Coders.

CODERS 1010

CODE 100

CODERS 0111

We need a plan.

A plan... listen. You know what happened to Josh's butt?

Hey!

What if we did the *same thing* to Cuddles?

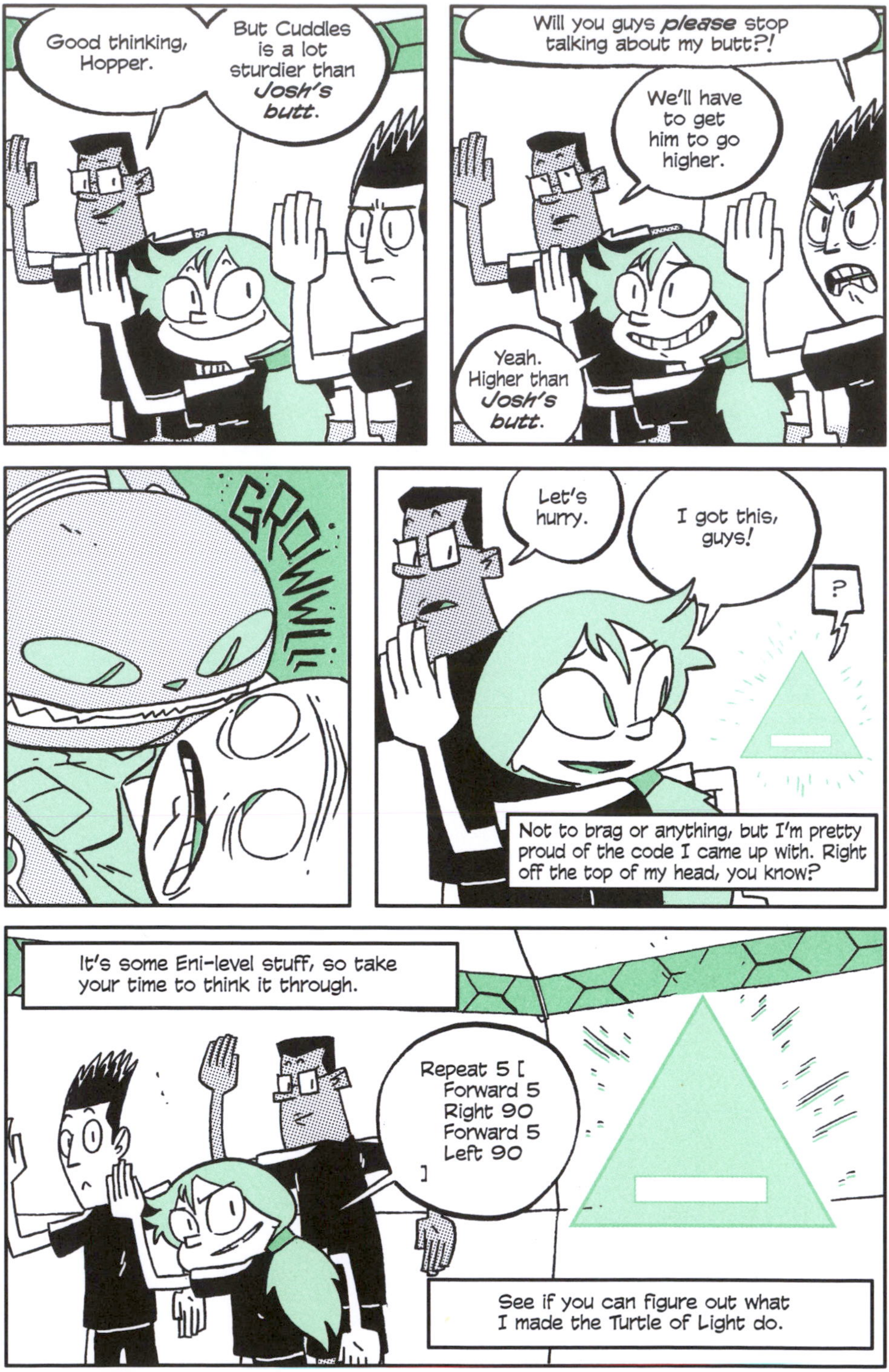

Good thinking, Hopper.
But Cuddles is a lot sturdier than *Josh's butt*.
Will you guys ***please*** stop talking about my butt?!
We'll have to get him to go higher.
Yeah. Higher than *Josh's butt*.
GROWWL!!
Let's hurry.
I got this, guys!
?
Not to brag or anything, but I'm pretty proud of the code I came up with. Right off the top of my head, you know?
It's some Eni-level stuff, so take your time to think it through.
Repeat 5 [
Forward 5
Right 90
Forward 5
Left 90
]
See if you can figure out what I made the Turtle of Light do.

Chapter

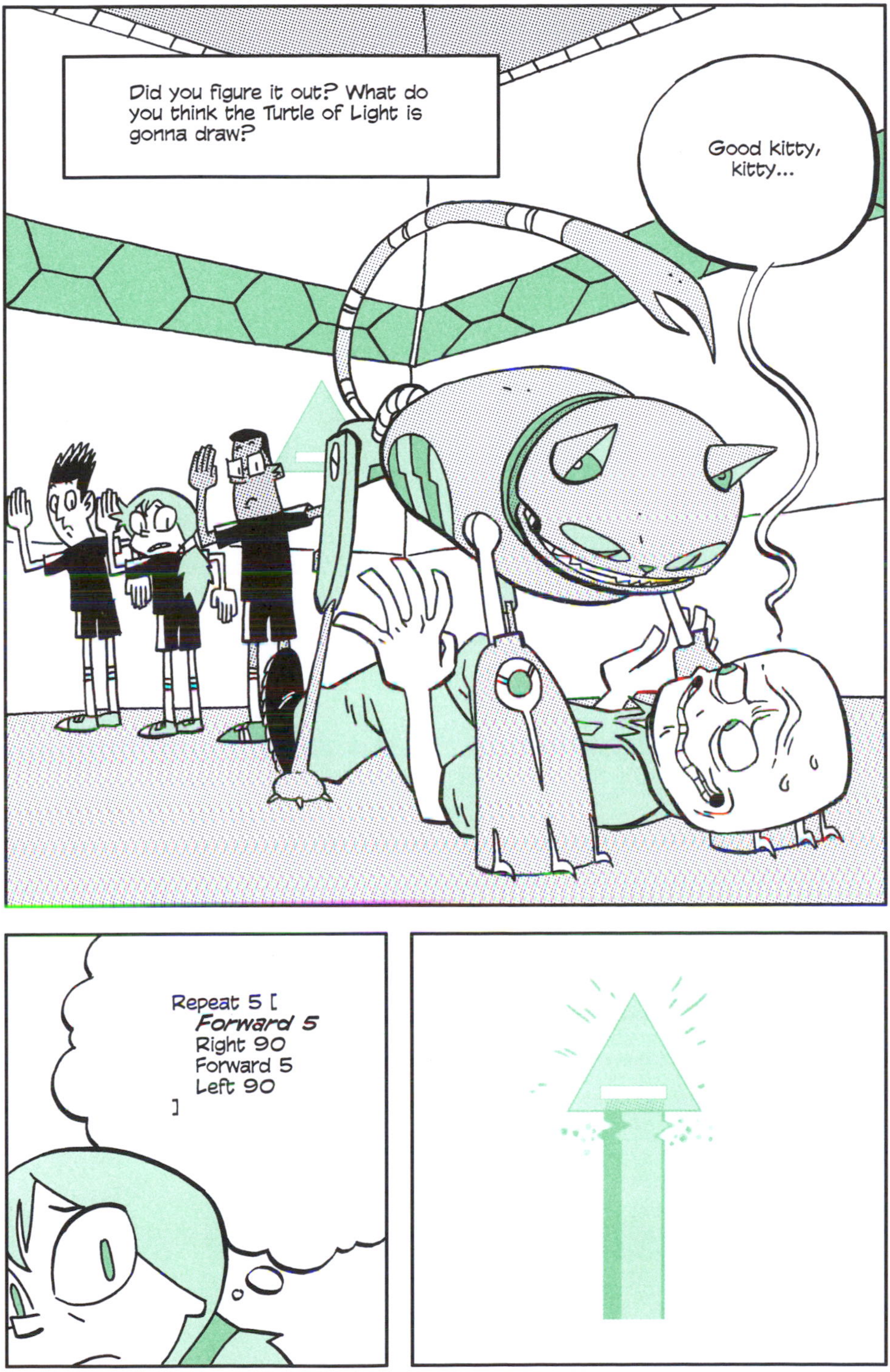
Did you figure it out? What do you think the Turtle of Light is gonna draw?
Good kitty, kitty...
Repeat 5 [
Forward 5
Right 90
Forward 5
Left 90
]

Repeat 5 [
 Forward 5
 Right 90
 Forward 5
 Left 90
]

Repeat 5 [
 Forward 5
 Right 90
 Forward 5
 Left 90
]

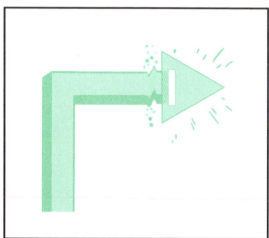

Repeat 5 [
 Forward 5
 Right 90
 Forward 5
 Left 90
]

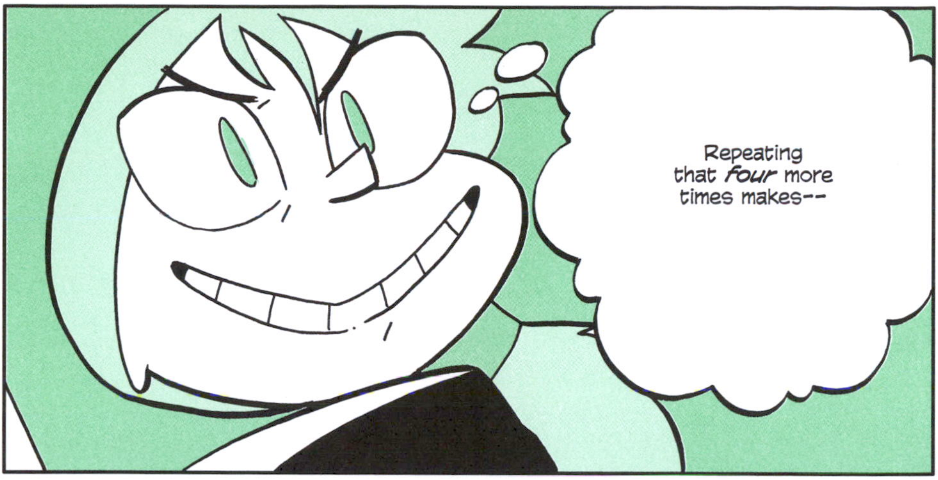
Repeating that *four* more times makes--

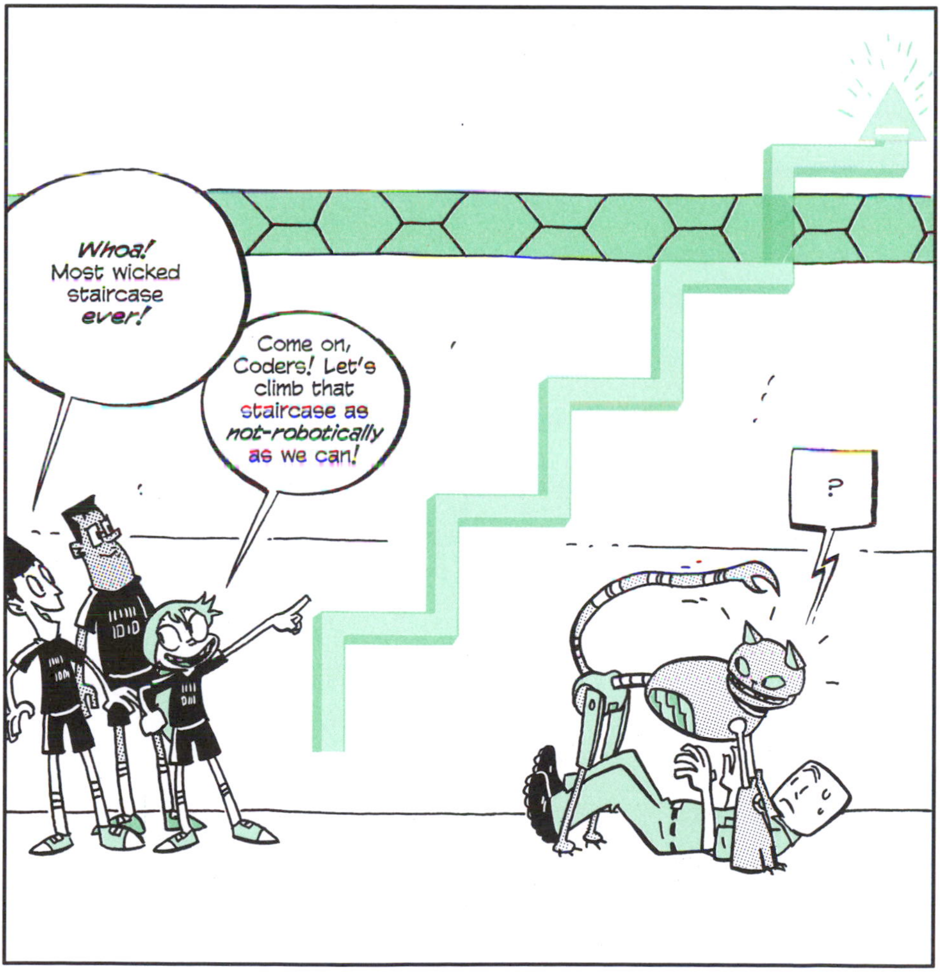
Whoa! Most wicked staircase *ever!*
Come on, Coders! Let's climb that staircase as *not-robotically* as we can!
?

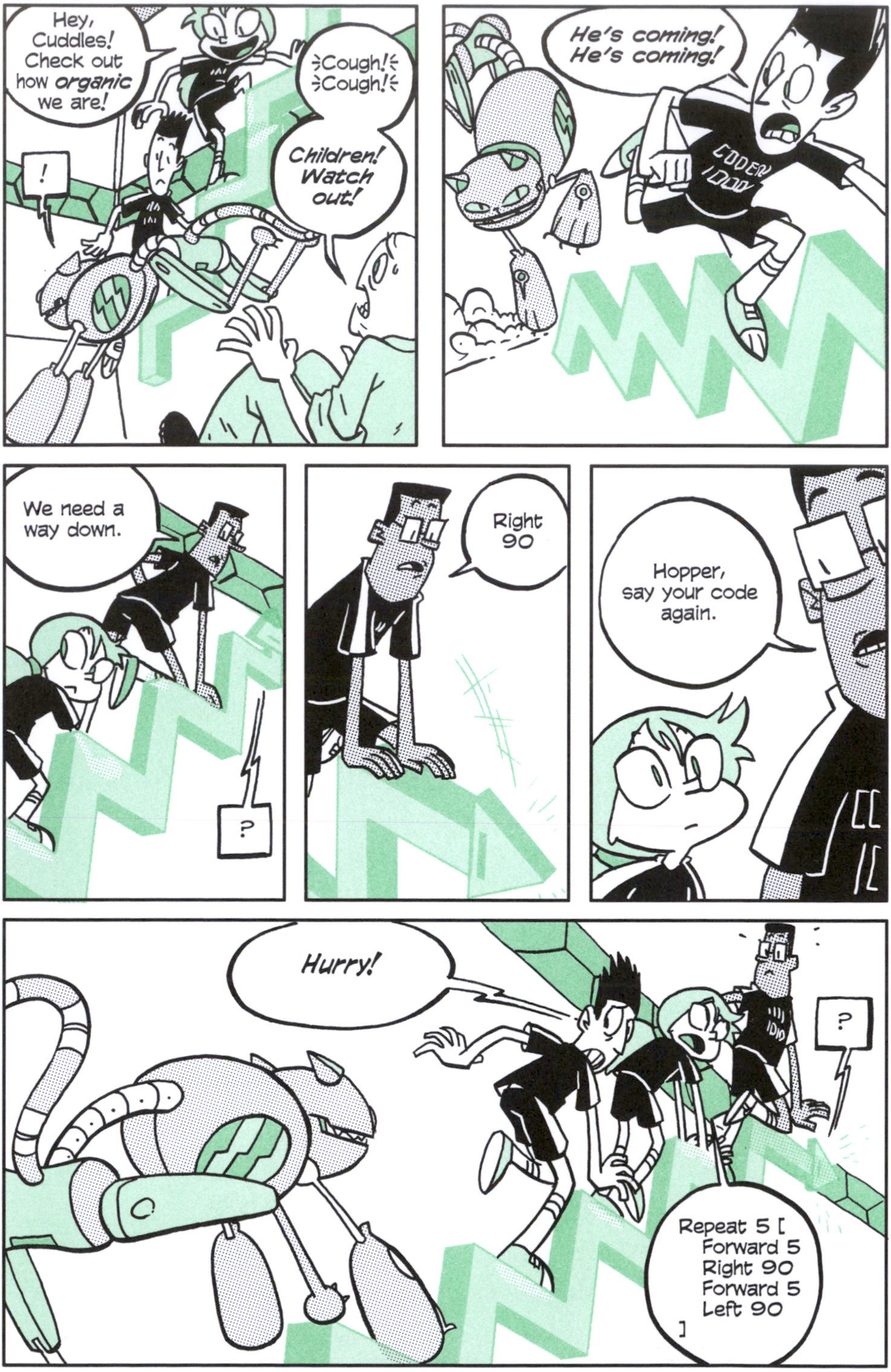
Hey, Cuddles! Check out how *organic* we are!
!
Cough! Cough!
Children! Watch out!
He's coming! He's coming!
We need a way down.
?
Right 90
Hopper, say your code again.
Hurry!
?
Repeat 5 [
Forward 5
Right 90
Forward 5
Left 90
]

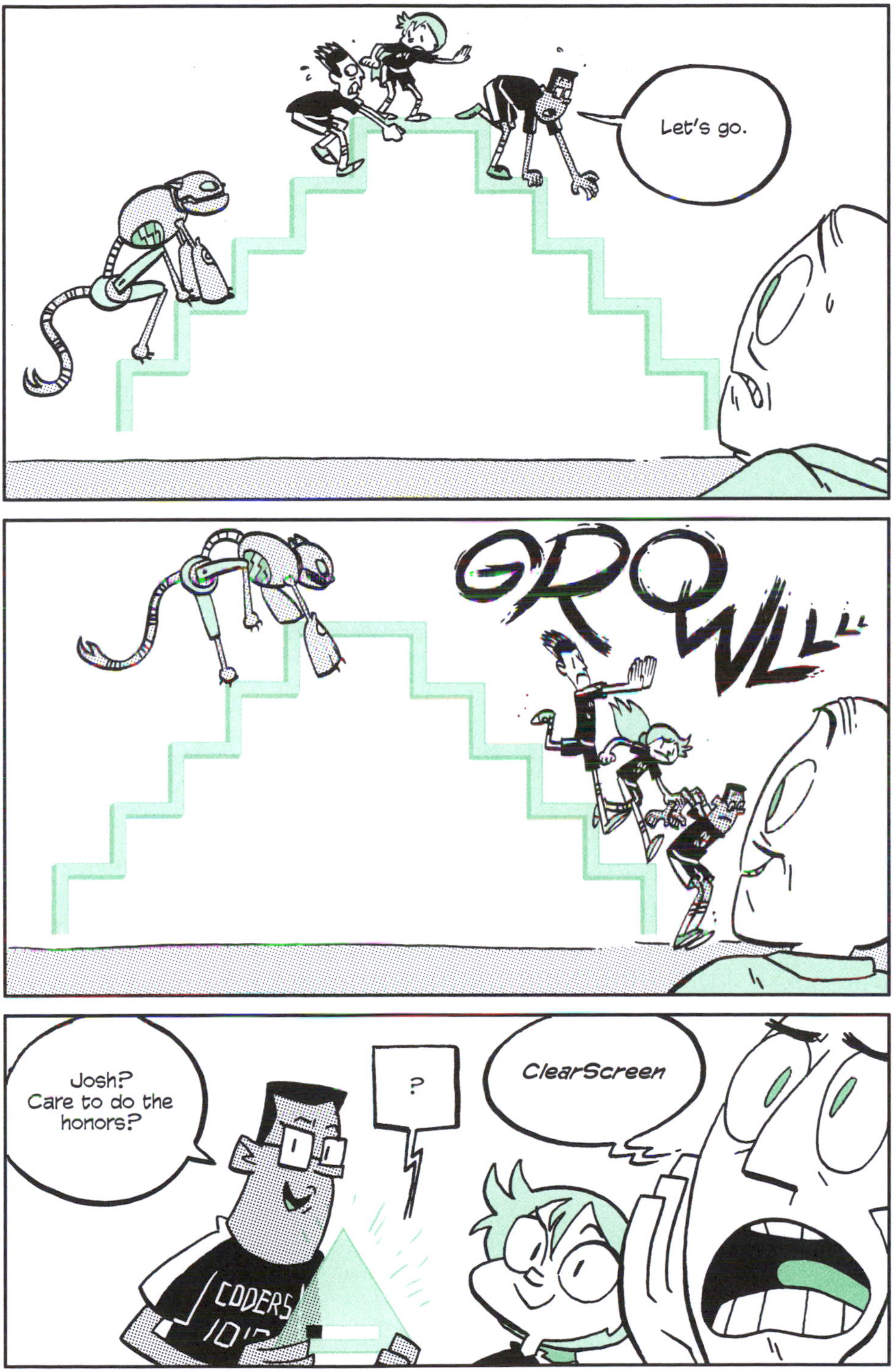
Let's go.
GROWL
Josh?
Care to do the honors?
?
ClearScreen
CODERS

CLERR!

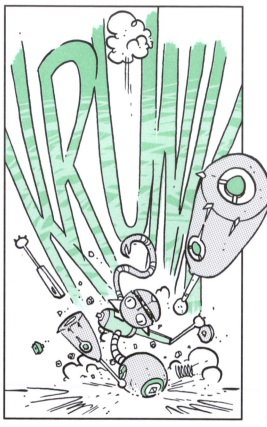

VRUW

Woohoo! ClearScreen rules!

Professor Bee! You're okay! Again!

Thanks to you all! My goodness, you've become such *accomplished coders!*

But not accomplished *enough*.

Professor Bee! I thought we were having a *moment* here!

Hopper, you said the same code twice. You could have used a Repeat instead.

But I *did* use a Repeat!

Yes, but you can use *more* than one in the same code, and you can *nest* them. Allow me to demonstrate.

Nest? Like a *bird*? We're dealing with *turtles* here, Professor!

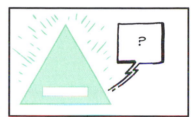

?

EdAll

I'm typing in Hopper's code and giving it the name *Staircase*.

```
To Staircase
Repeat 5 [
   Forward 5
   Right 90
   Forward 5
   Left 90
]
End
```

The Turtle of Light has its own keyboard?

Keyboard of Light!

25

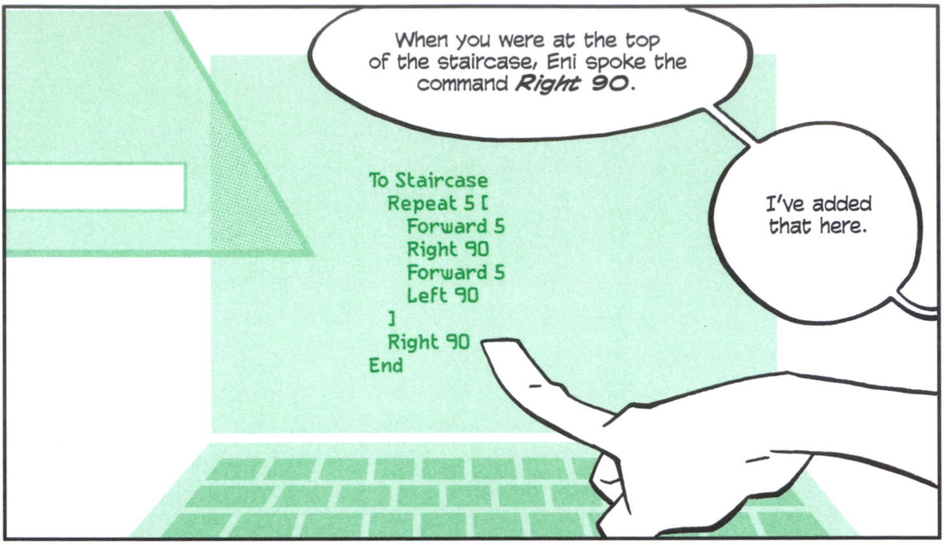
When you were at the top of the staircase, Eni spoke the command *Right 90*.
I've added that here.
To Staircase
Repeat 5 [
Forward 5
Right 90
Forward 5
Left 90
]
Right 90
End

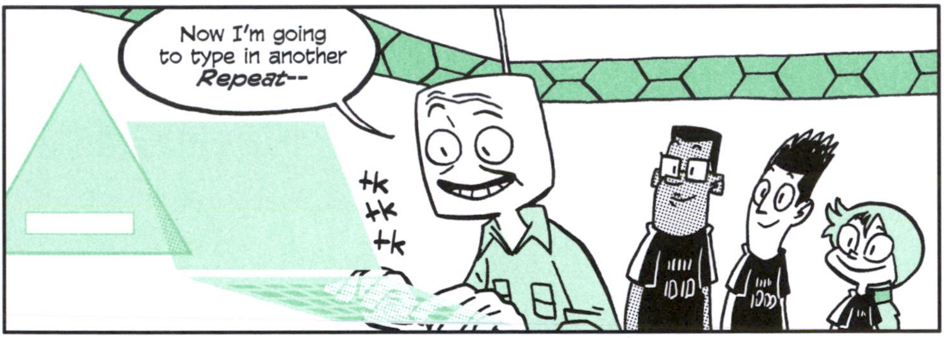
Now I'm going to type in another *Repeat*--
tk
tk
tk

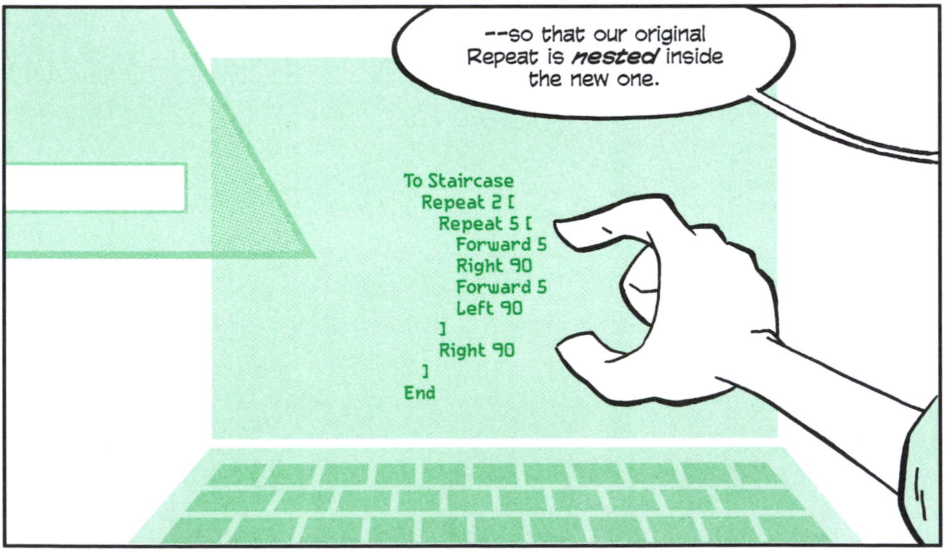
--so that our original Repeat is *nested* inside the new one.
To Staircase
Repeat 2 [
Repeat 5 [
Forward 5
Right 90
Forward 5
Left 90
]
Right 90
]
End

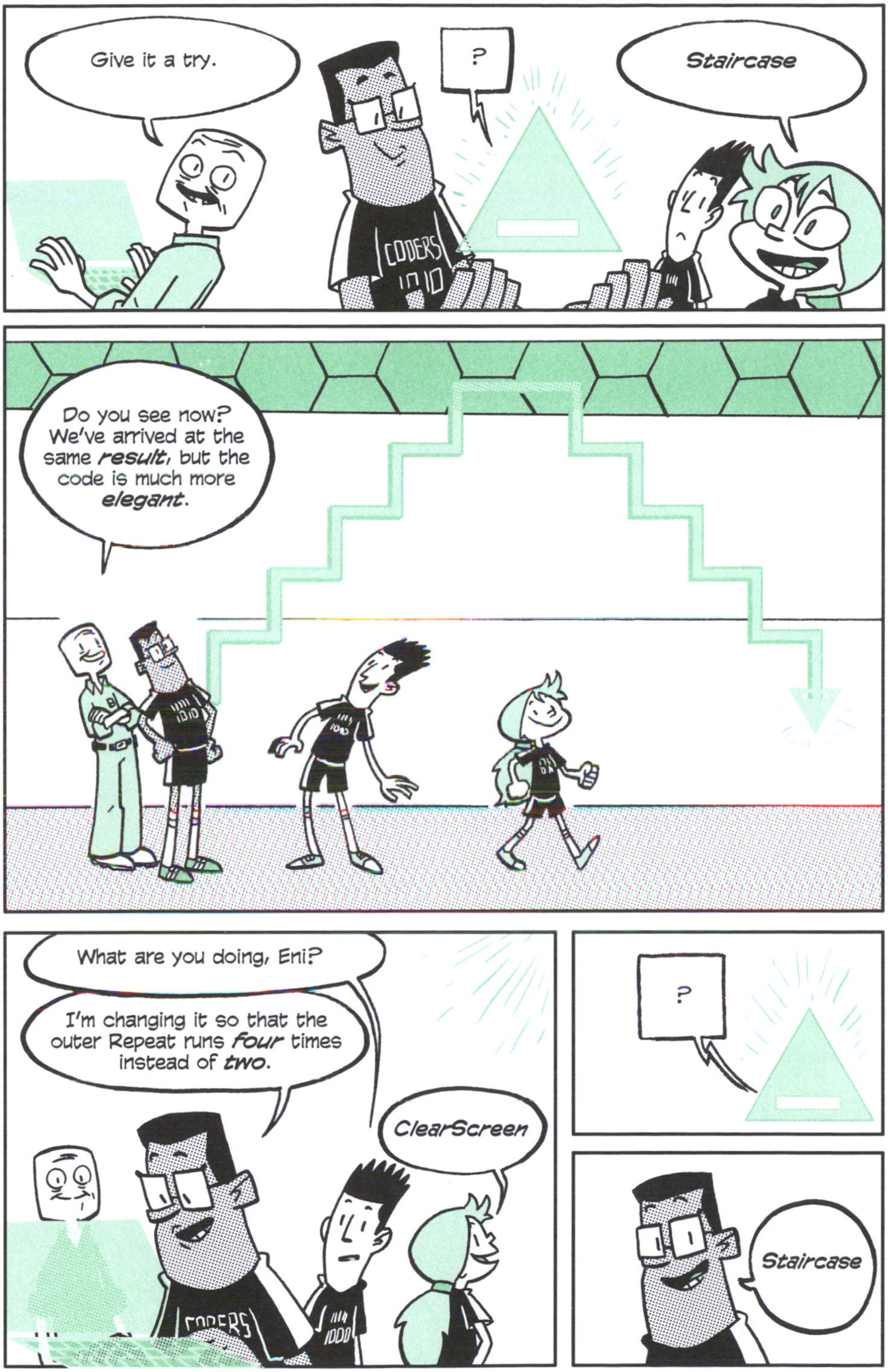
Give it a try.
?
Staircase
Do you see now? We've arrived at the same *result*, but the code is much more *elegant*.
What are you doing, Eni?
I'm changing it so that the outer Repeat runs *four* times instead of *two*.
ClearScreen
?
Staircase

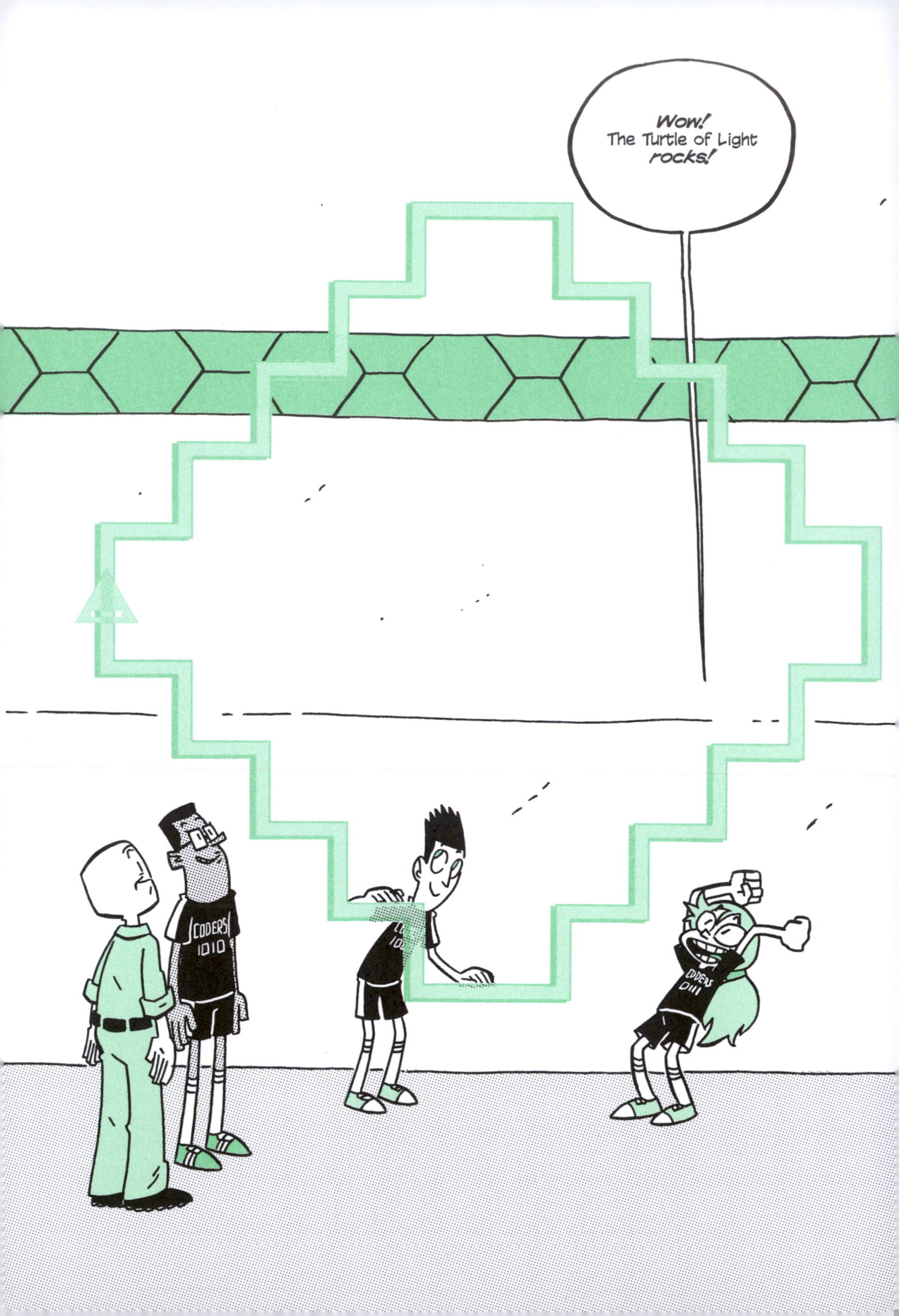
Wow! The Turtle of Light rocks!
CODERS 1010
CODERS 0111

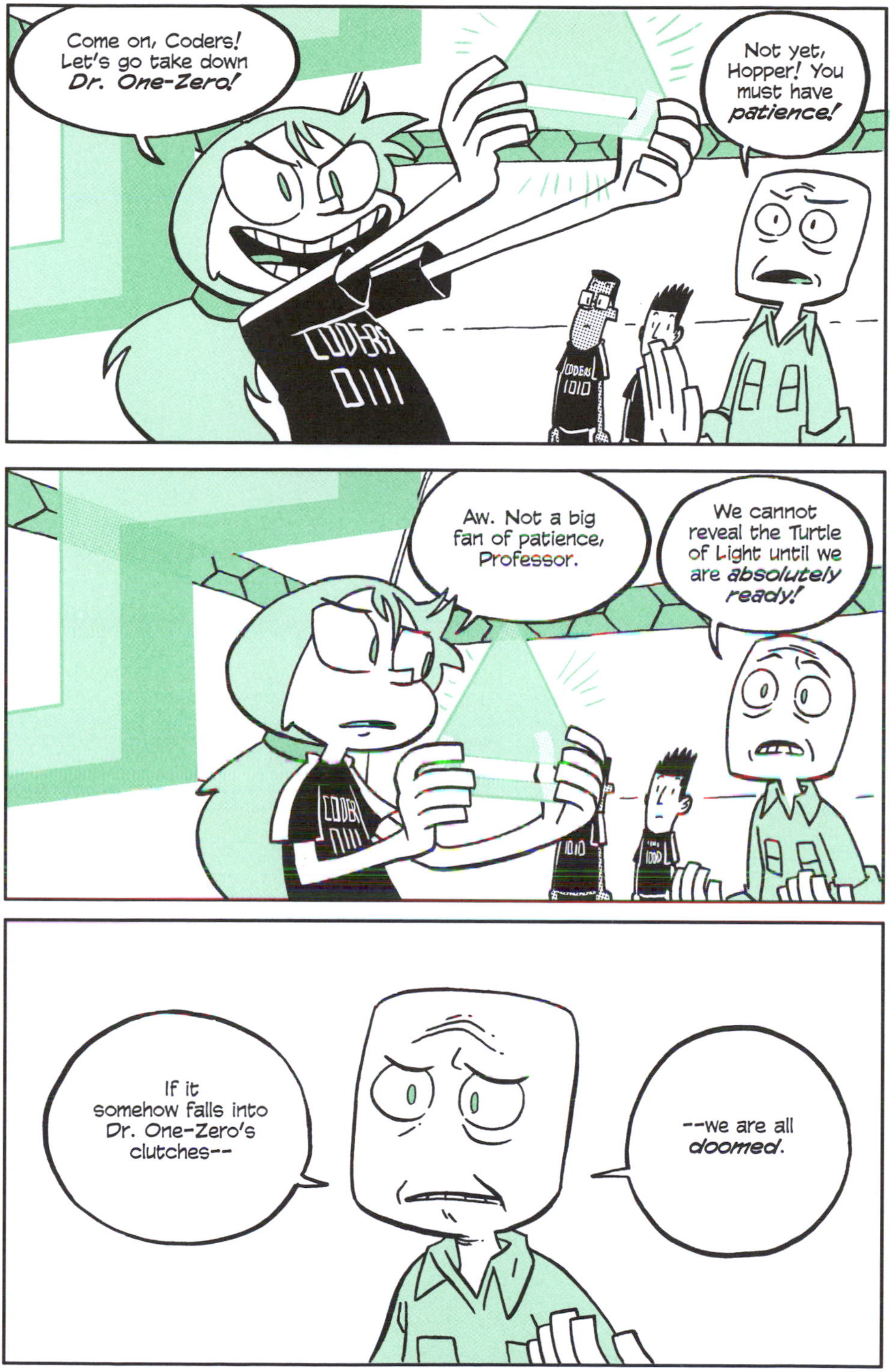
Come on, Coders! Let's go take down *Dr. One-Zero!*
Not yet, Hopper! You must have *patience!*
CODERS 0111
CODERS 1010
Aw. Not a big fan of patience, Professor.
We cannot reveal the Turtle of Light until we are *absolutely ready!*
If it somehow falls into Dr. One-Zero's clutches--
--we are all *doomed*.

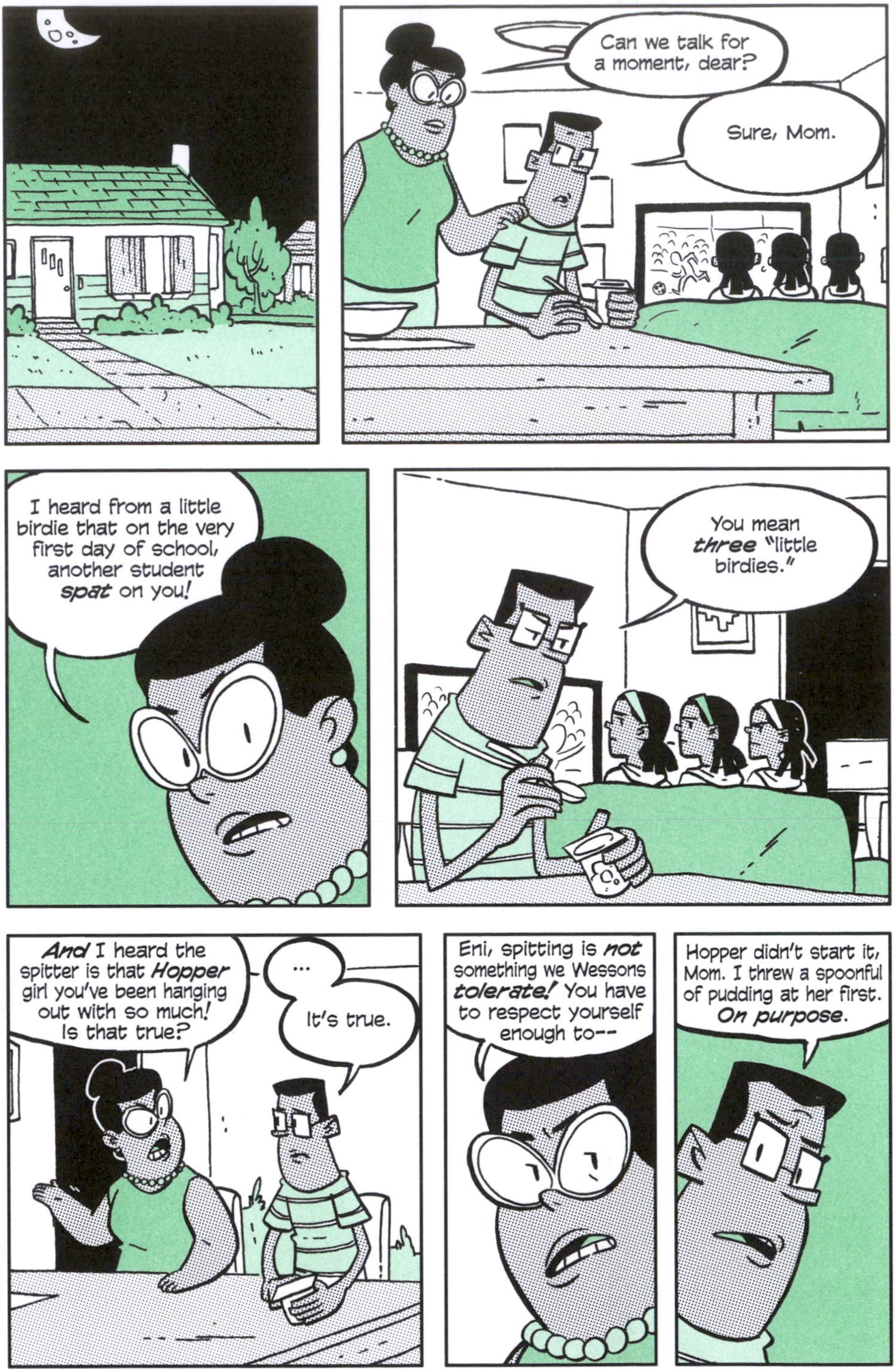
Can we talk for a moment, dear?
Sure, Mom.
I heard from a little birdie that on the very first day of school, another student *spat* on you!
You mean *three* "little birdies."
And I heard the spitter is that *Hopper* girl you've been hanging out with so much! Is that true?
...
It's true.
Eni, spitting is *not* something we Wessons *tolerate!* You have to respect yourself enough to--
Hopper didn't start it, Mom. I threw a spoonful of pudding at her first. *On purpose*.

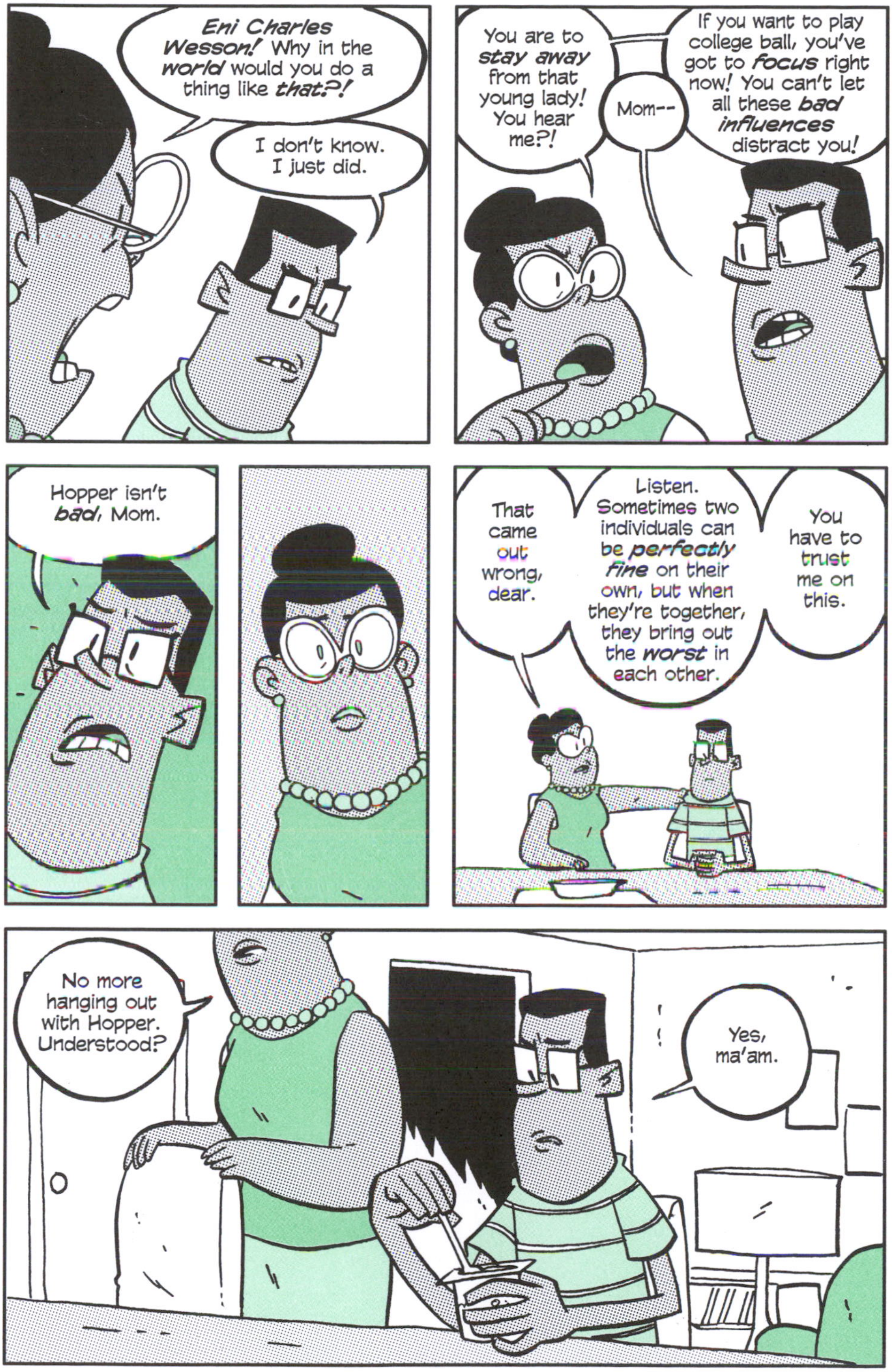

Eni Charles Wesson! Why in the world would you do a thing like that?!
I don't know. I just did.
You are to stay away from that young lady! You hear me?!
Mom--
If you want to play college ball, you've got to focus right now! You can't let all these bad influences distract you!
Hopper isn't bad, Mom.
That came out wrong, dear.
Listen. Sometimes two individuals can be perfectly fine on their own, but when they're together, they bring out the worst in each other.
You have to trust me on this.
No more hanging out with Hopper. Understood?
Yes, ma'am.

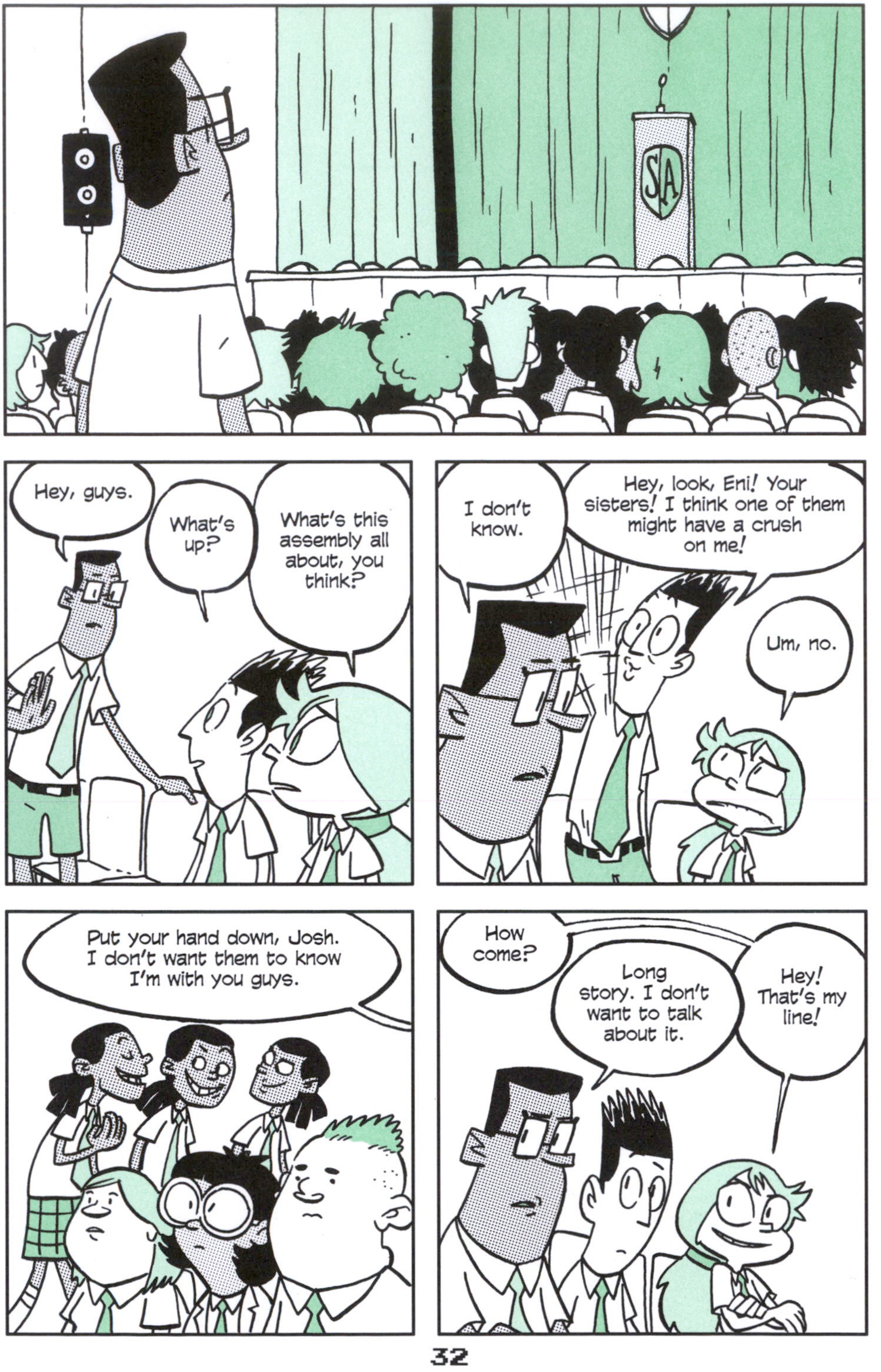
Hey, guys.
What's up?
What's this assembly all about, you think?
I don't know.
Hey, look, Eni! Your sisters! I think one of them might have a crush on me!
Um, no.
Put your hand down, Josh. I don't want them to know I'm with you guys.
How come?
Long story. I don't want to talk about it.
Hey! That's my line!

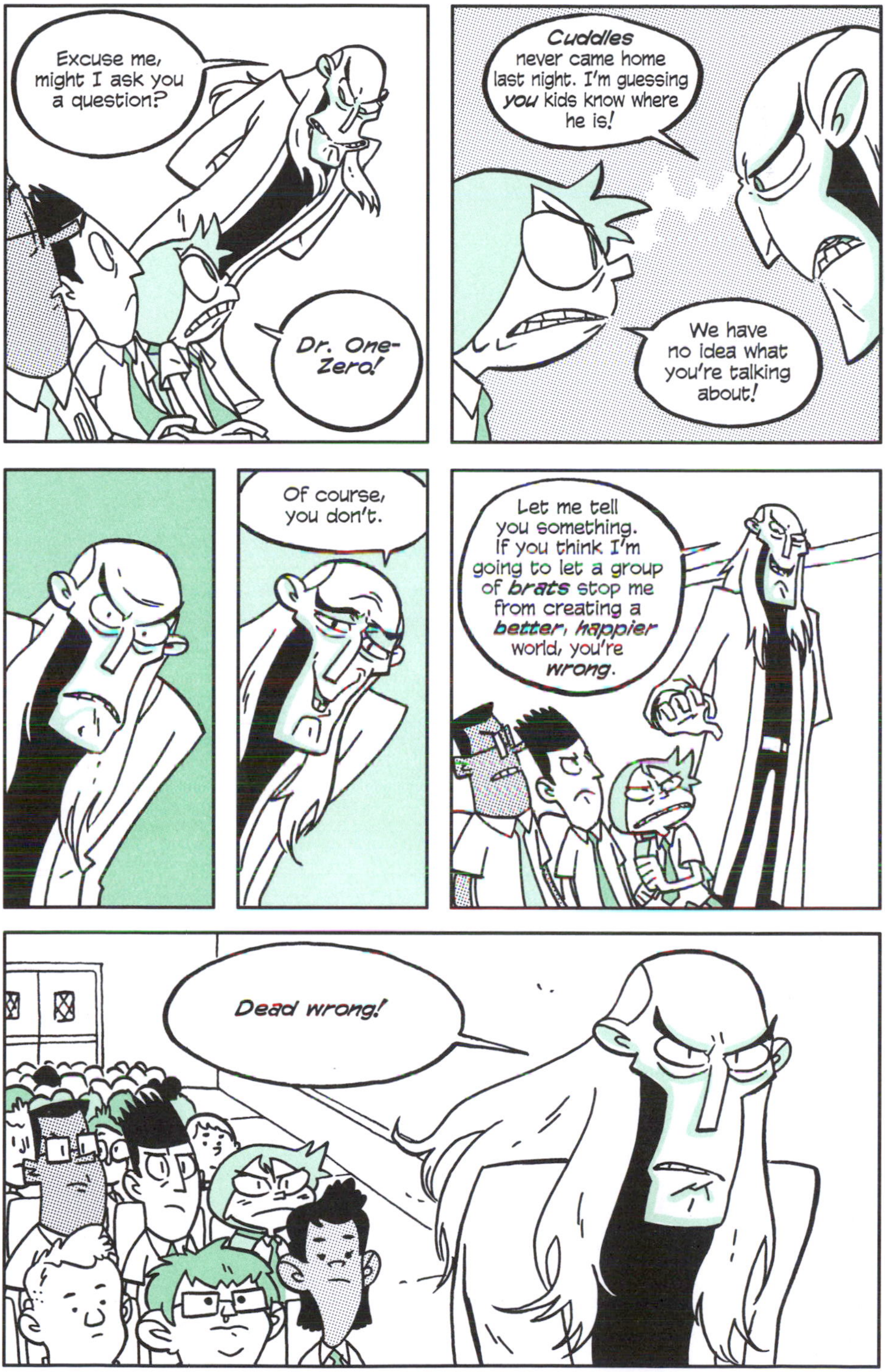
Excuse me, might I ask you a question?
Dr. One-Zero!
Cuddles never came home last night. I'm guessing you kids know where he is!
We have no idea what you're talking about!
Of course, you don't.
Let me tell you something. If you think I'm going to let a group of brats stop me from creating a better, happier world, you're wrong.
Dead wrong!

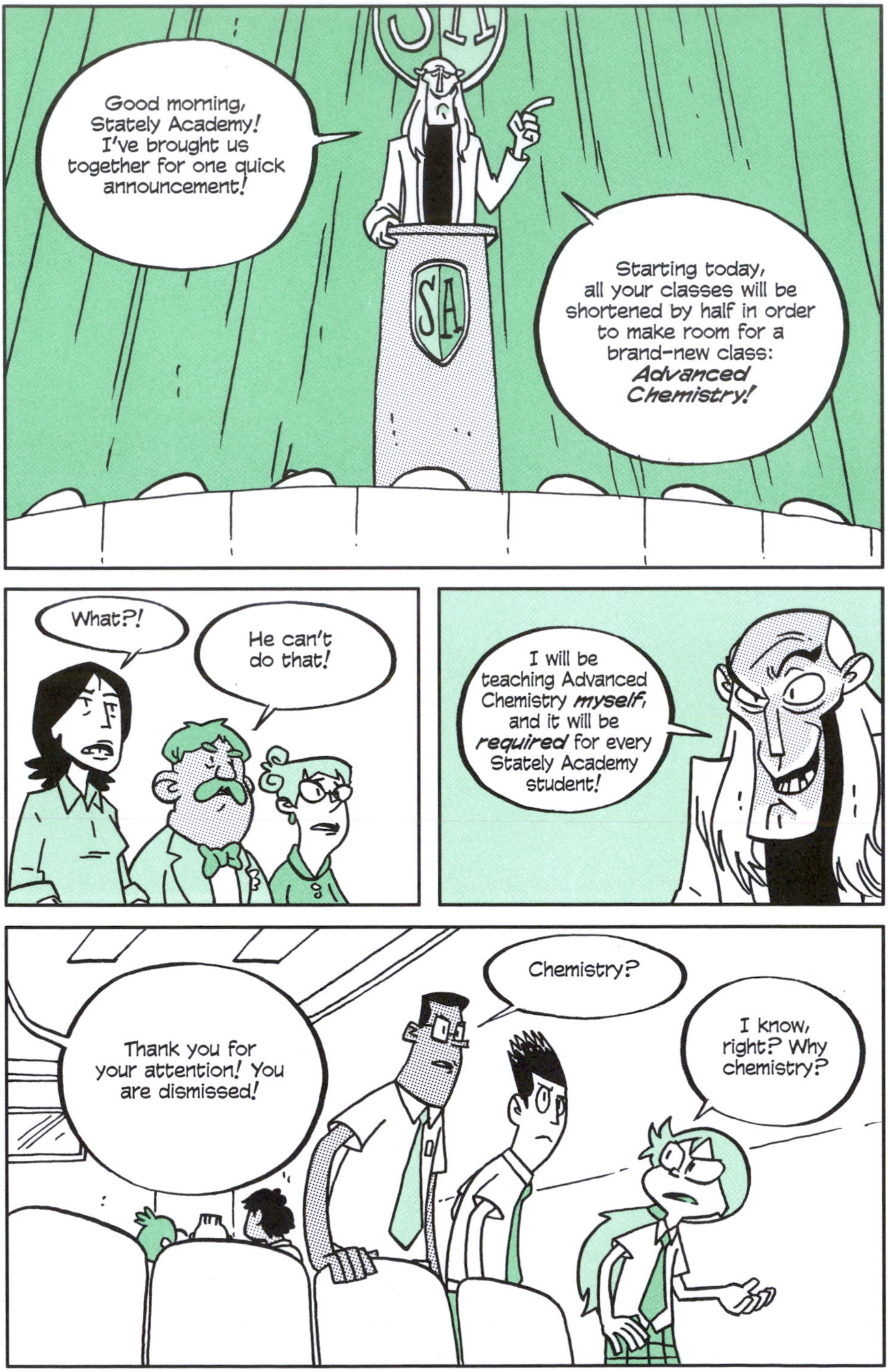
Good morning, Stately Academy! I've brought us together for one quick announcement!
Starting today, all your classes will be shortened by half in order to make room for a brand-new class: *Advanced Chemistry!*
What?!
He can't do that!
I will be teaching Advanced Chemistry *myself*, and it will be *required* for every Stately Academy student!
Thank you for your attention! You are dismissed!
Chemistry?
I know, right? Why chemistry?

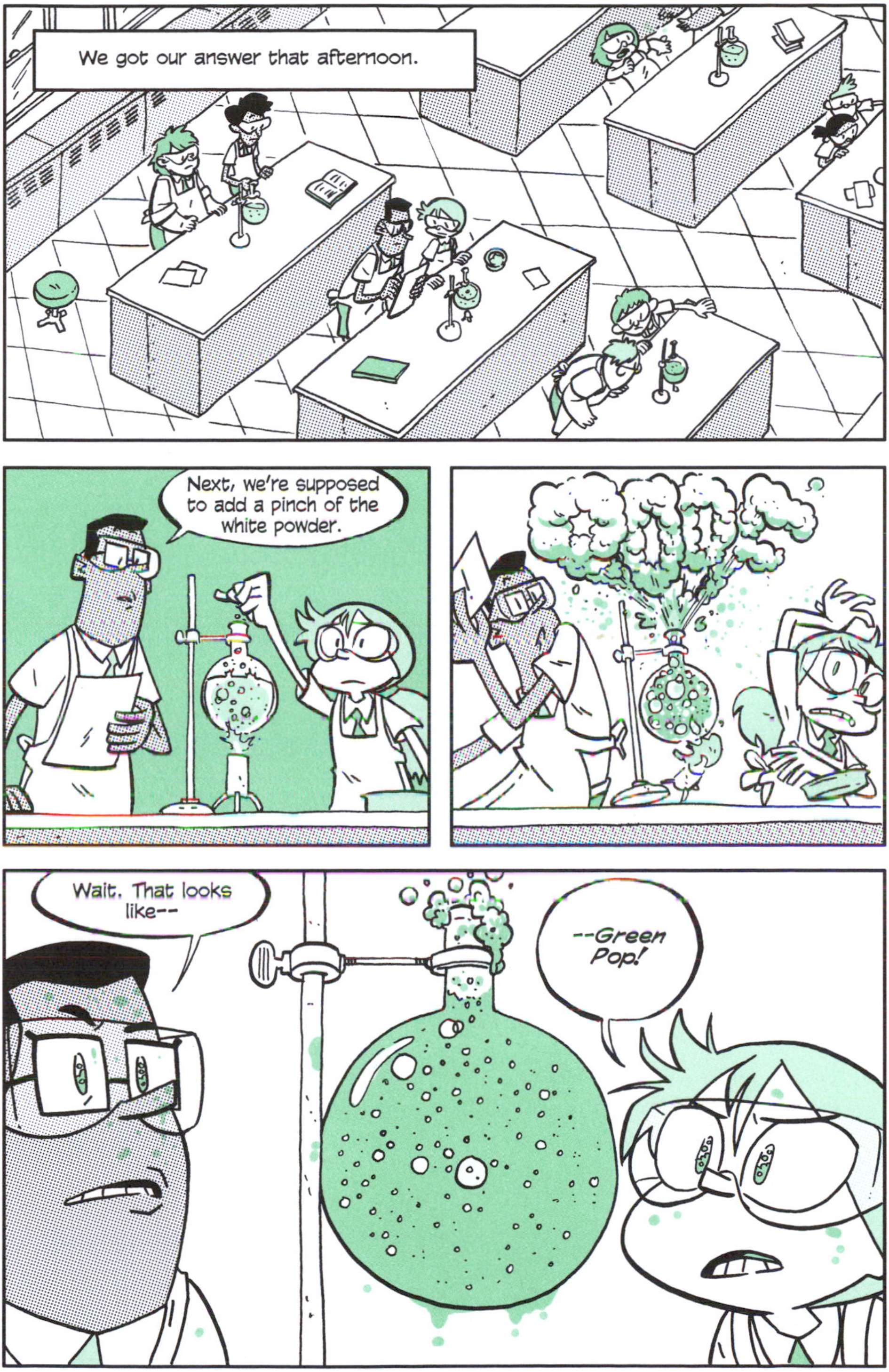
We got our answer that afternoon.
Next, we're supposed to add a pinch of the white powder.
Wait. That looks like--
--Green Pop!

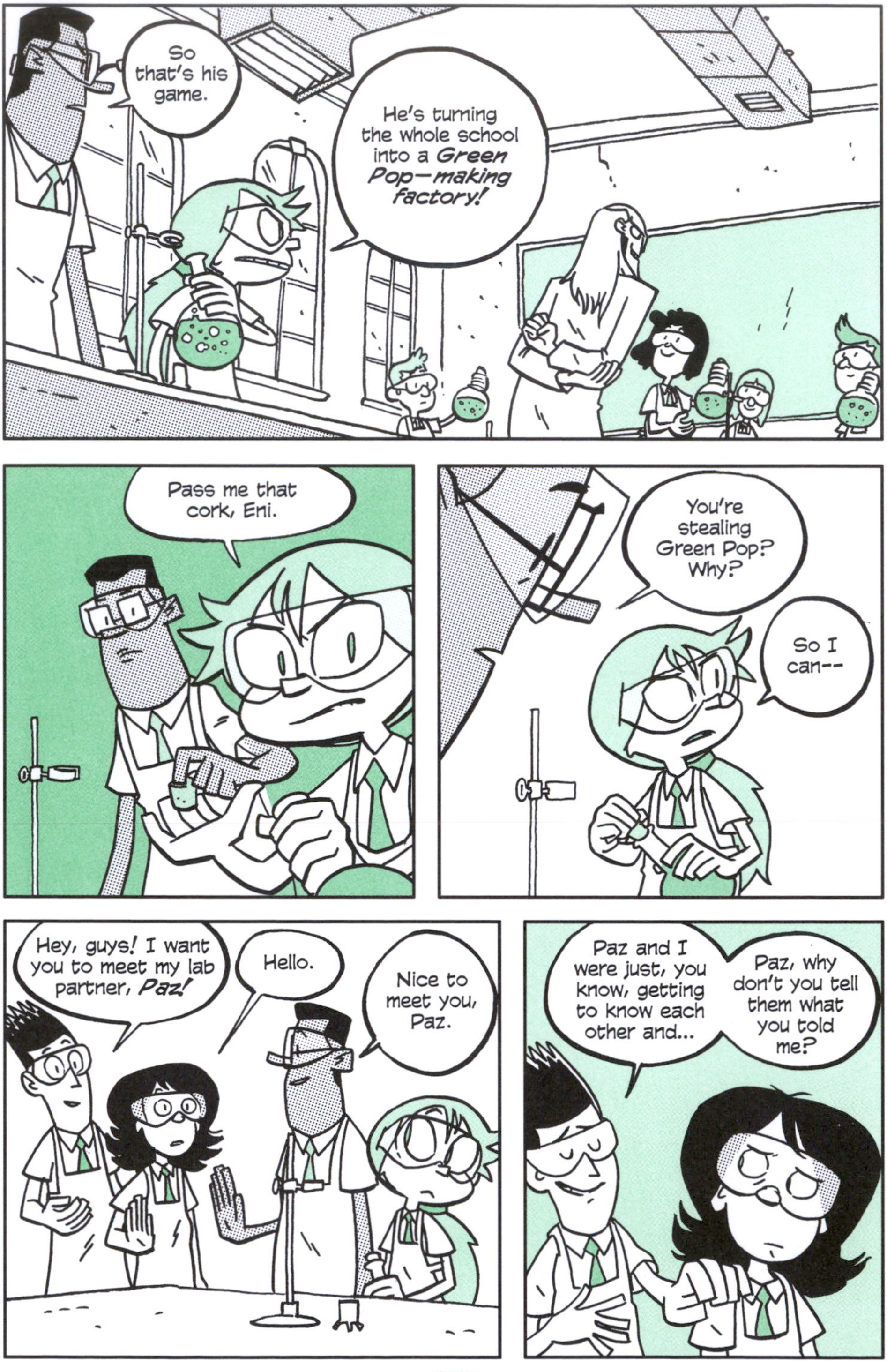

So that's his game.
He's turning the whole school into a *Green Pop—making factory!*
Pass me that cork, Eni.
You're stealing Green Pop? Why?
So I can--
Hey, guys! I want you to meet my lab partner, *Paz!*
Hello.
Nice to meet you, Paz.
Paz and I were just, you know, getting to know each other and...
Paz, why don't you tell them what you told me?

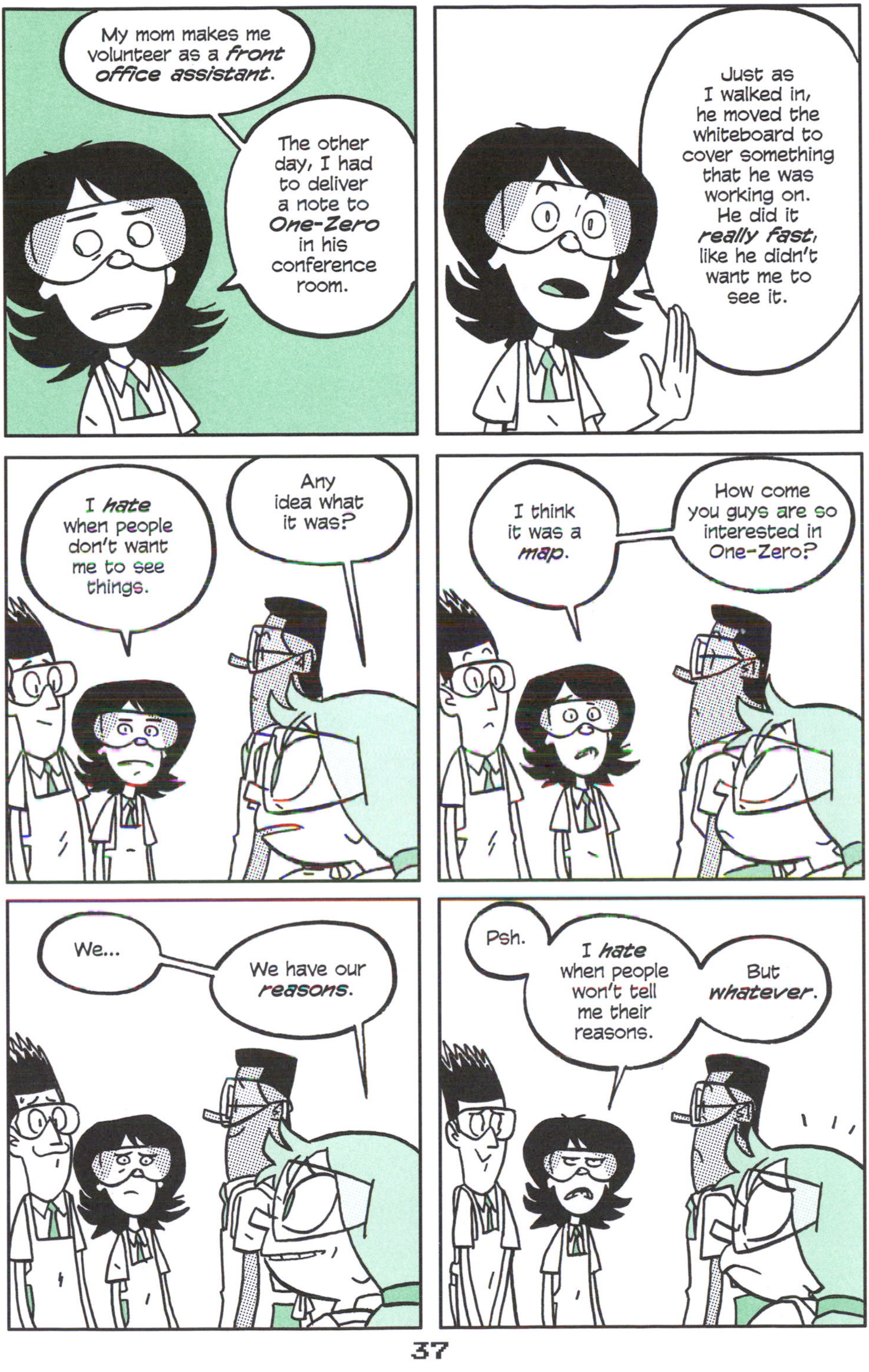
My mom makes me volunteer as a *front office assistant*.
The other day, I had to deliver a note to *One-Zero* in his conference room.
Just as I walked in, he moved the whiteboard to cover something that he was working on. He did it *really fast*, like he didn't want me to see it.
I *hate* when people don't want me to see things.
Any idea what it was?
I think it was a *map*.
How come you guys are so interested in One-Zero?
We...
We have our *reasons*.
Psh.
I *hate* when people won't tell me their reasons.
But *whatever*.

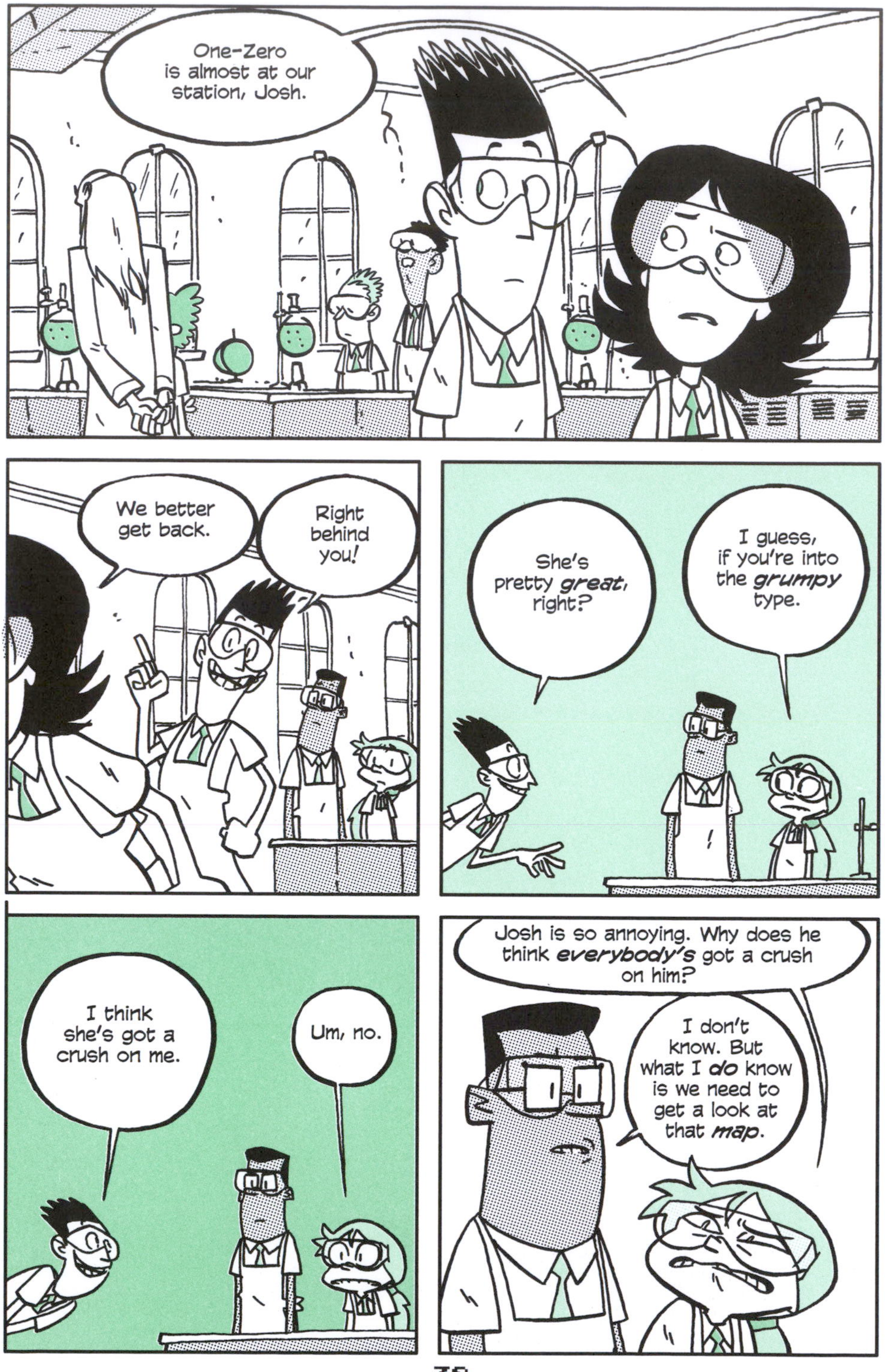
One-Zero is almost at our station, Josh.
We better get back.
Right behind you!
She's pretty *great*, right?
I guess, if you're into the *grumpy* type.
I think she's got a crush on me.
Um, no.
Josh is so annoying. Why does he think *everybody's* got a crush on him?
I don't know. But what I *do* know is we need to get a look at that *map*.

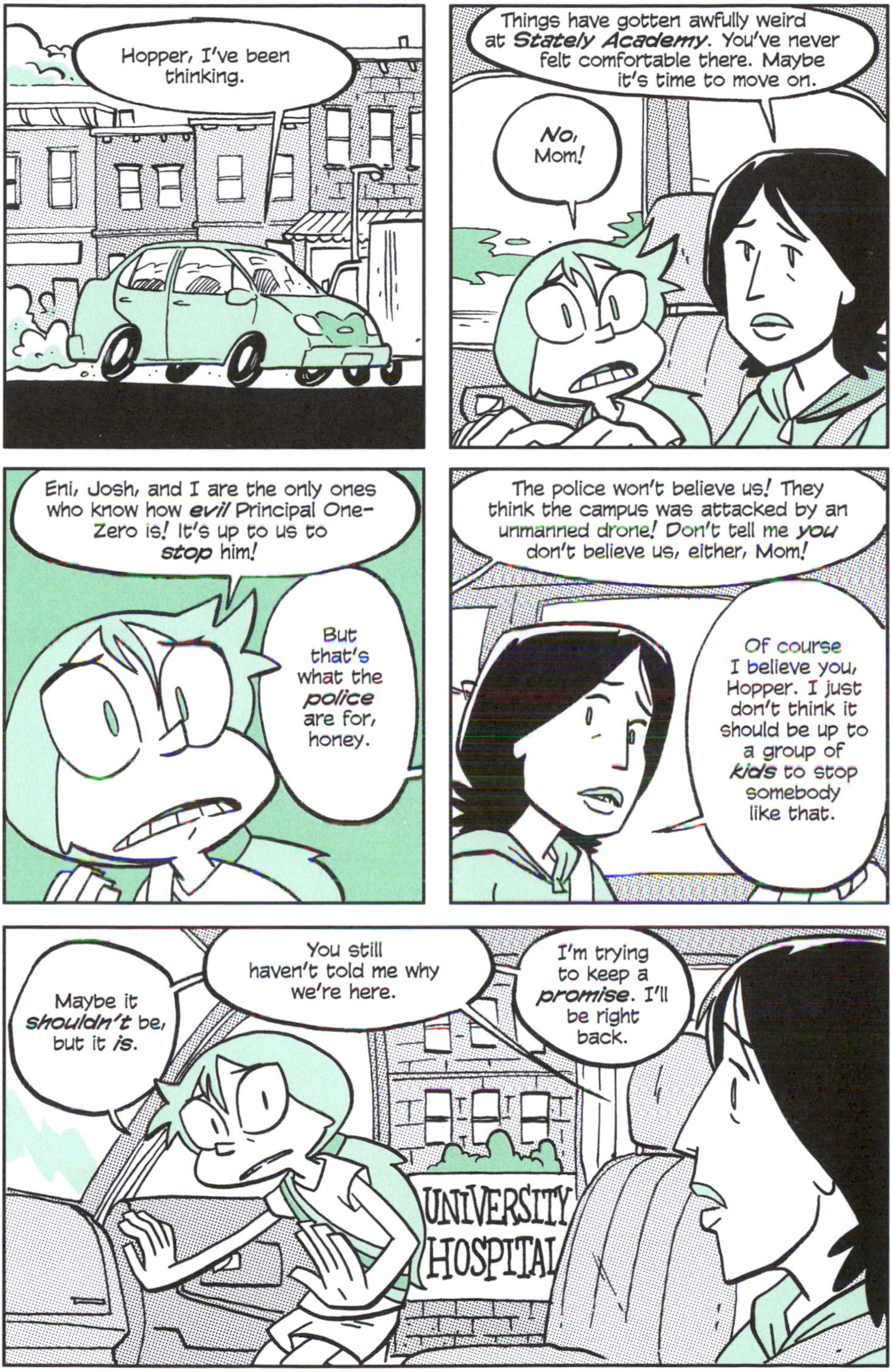
Hopper, I've been thinking.
Things have gotten awfully weird at *Stately Academy*. You've never felt comfortable there. Maybe it's time to move on.
No, Mom!
Eni, Josh, and I are the only ones who know how *evil* Principal One-Zero is! It's up to us to *stop* him!
But that's what the *police* are for, honey.
The police won't believe us! They think the campus was attacked by an unmanned drone! Don't tell me *you* don't believe us, either, Mom!
Of course I believe you, Hopper. I just don't think it should be up to a group of *kids* to stop somebody like that.
Maybe it *shouldn't* be, but it *is*.
You still haven't told me why we're here.
I'm trying to keep a *promise*. I'll be right back.
UNIVERSITY HOSPITAL

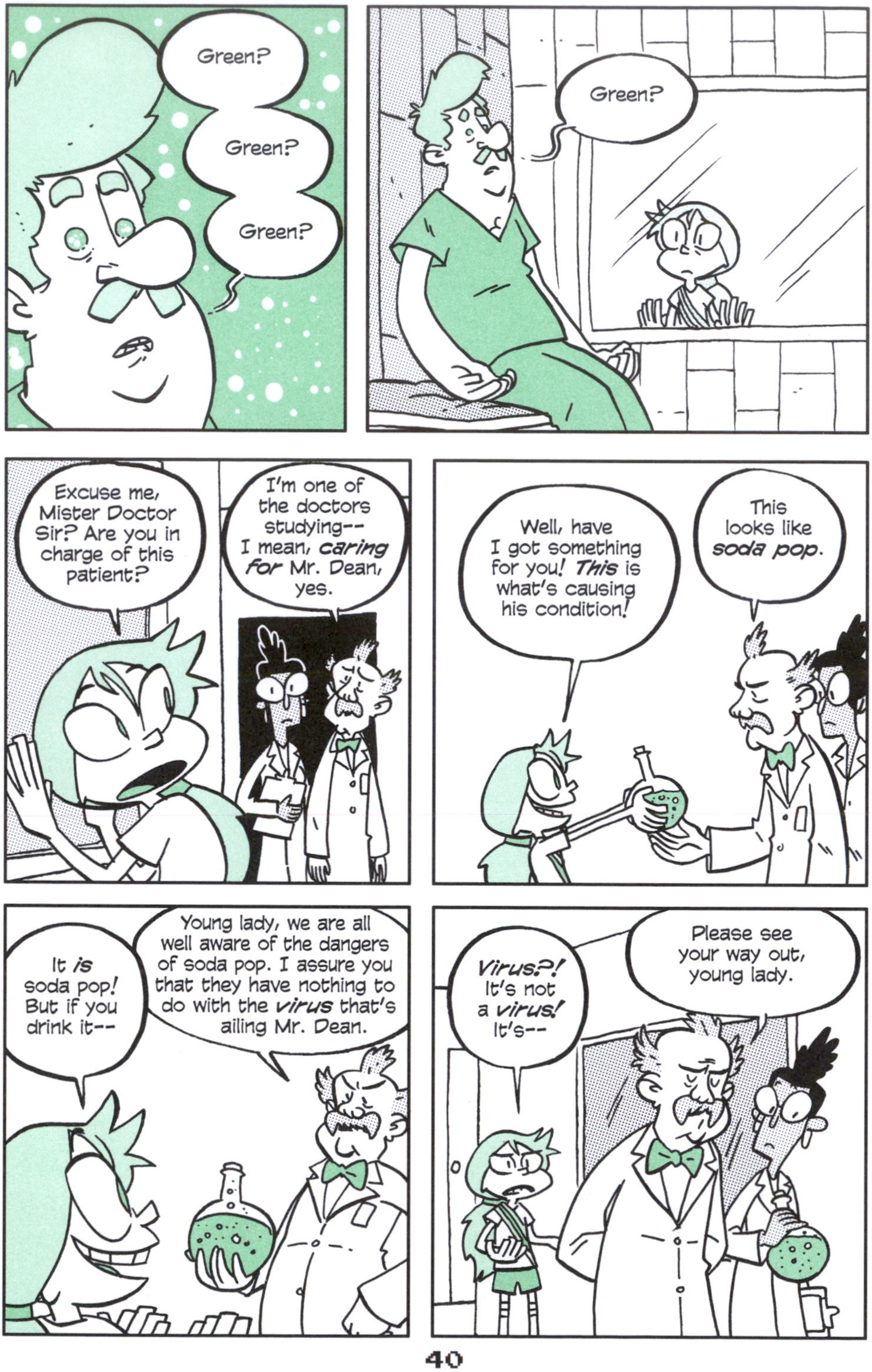
Green?
Green?
Green?
Green?
Excuse me, Mister Doctor Sir? Are you in charge of this patient?
I'm one of the doctors studying-- I mean, *caring for* Mr. Dean, yes.
Well, have I got something for you! *This* is what's causing his condition!
This looks like *soda pop*.
It *is* soda pop! But if you drink it--
Young lady, we are all well aware of the dangers of soda pop. I assure you that they have nothing to do with the *virus* that's ailing Mr. Dean.
Virus?! It's not a *virus!* It's--
Please see your way out, young lady.

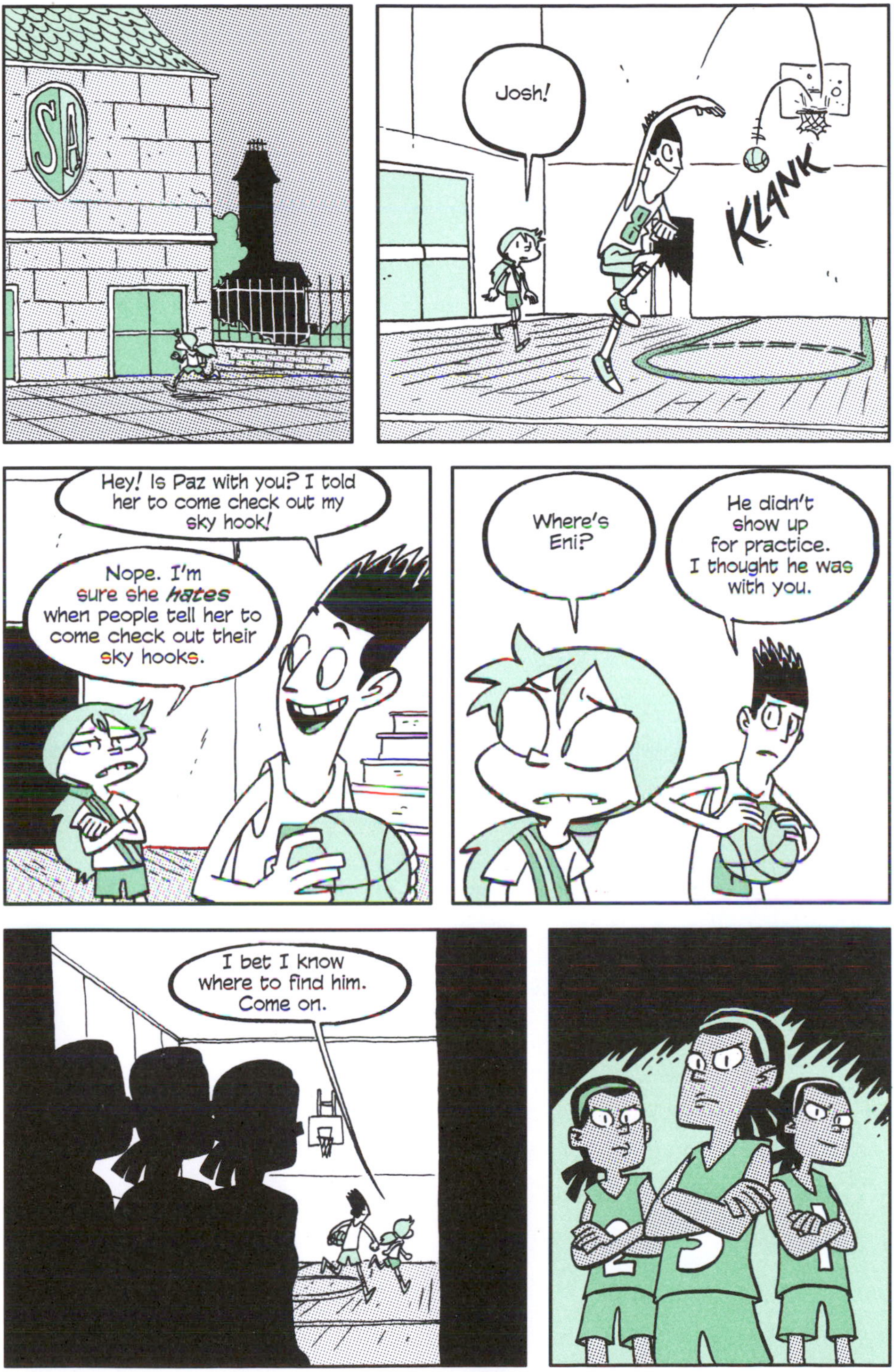
Josh!
KLANK
Hey! Is Paz with you? I told her to come check out my sky hook!
Nope. I'm sure she *hates* when people tell her to come check out their sky hooks.
Where's Eni?
He didn't show up for practice. I thought he was with you.
I bet I know where to find him. Come on.

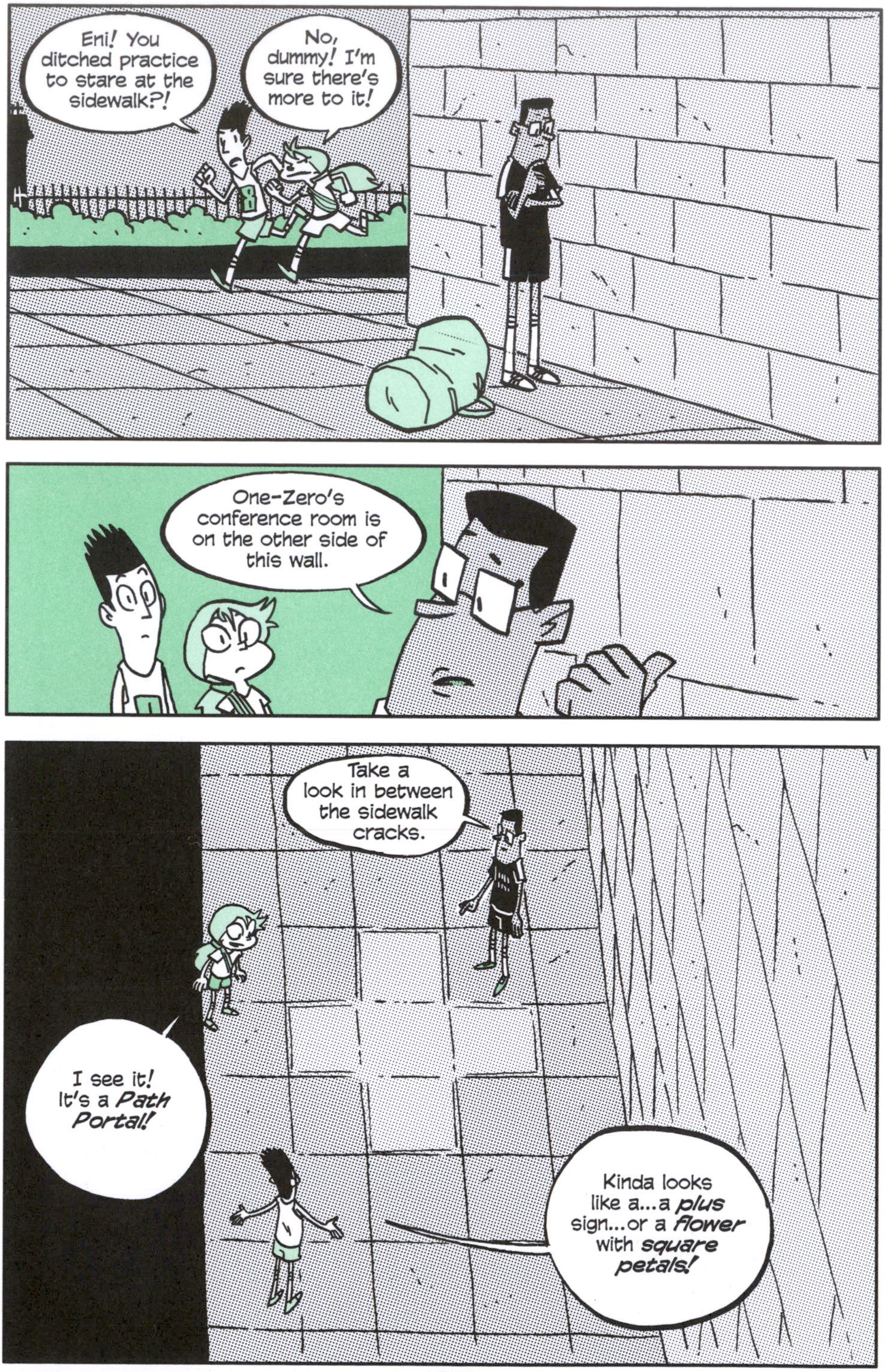
Eni! You ditched practice to stare at the sidewalk?!
No, dummy! I'm sure there's more to it!
One-Zero's conference room is on the other side of this wall.
Take a look in between the sidewalk cracks.
I see it! It's a *Path Portal!*
Kinda looks like a...a *plus* sign...or a *flower* with *square petals!*

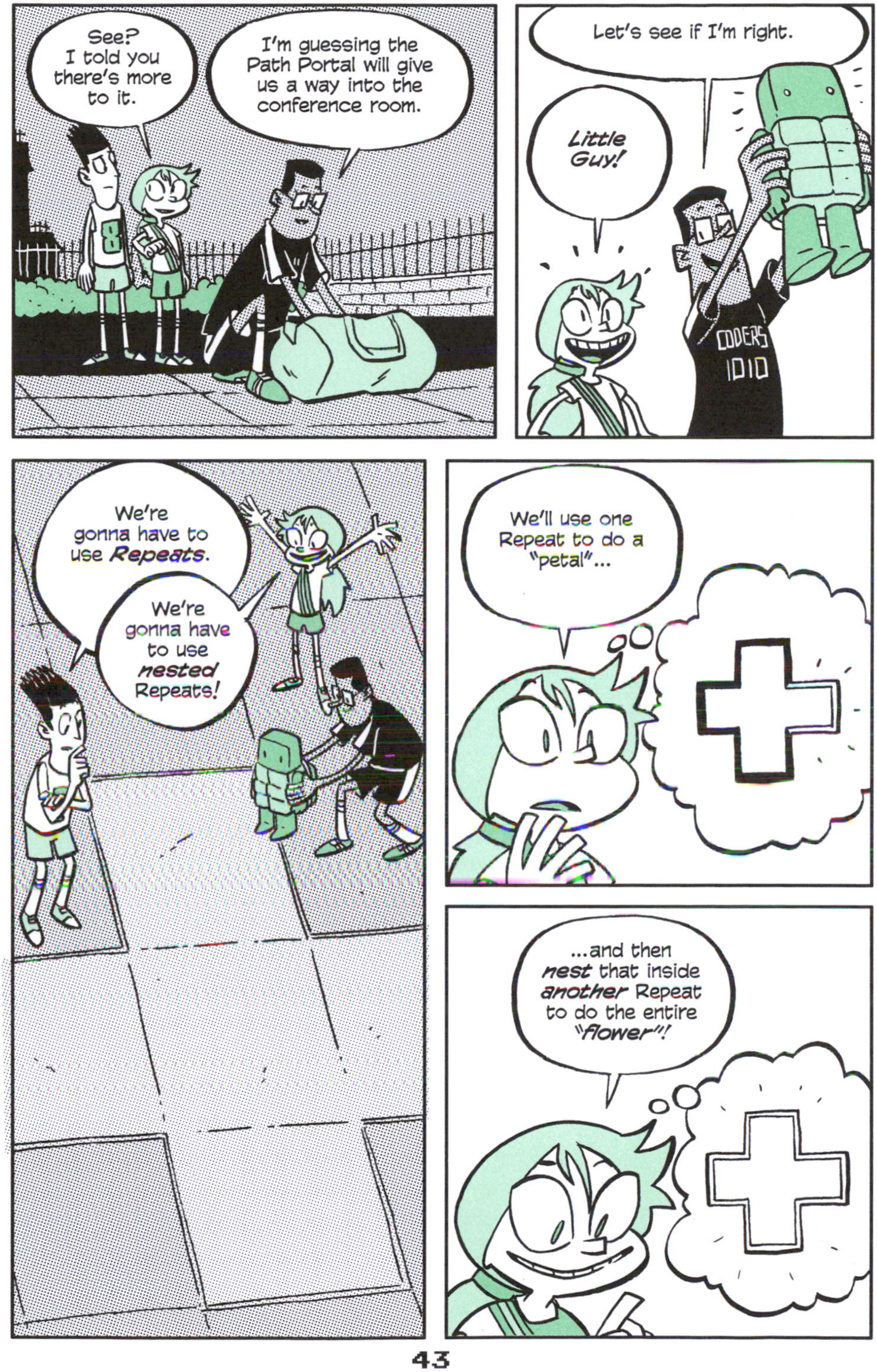

See? I told you there's more to it.
I'm guessing the Path Portal will give us a way into the conference room.
Let's see if I'm right.
Little Guy!
CODERS 1010
We're gonna have to use Repeats.
We're gonna have to use nested Repeats!
We'll use one Repeat to do a "petal"...
...and then nest that inside another Repeat to do the entire "flower"!

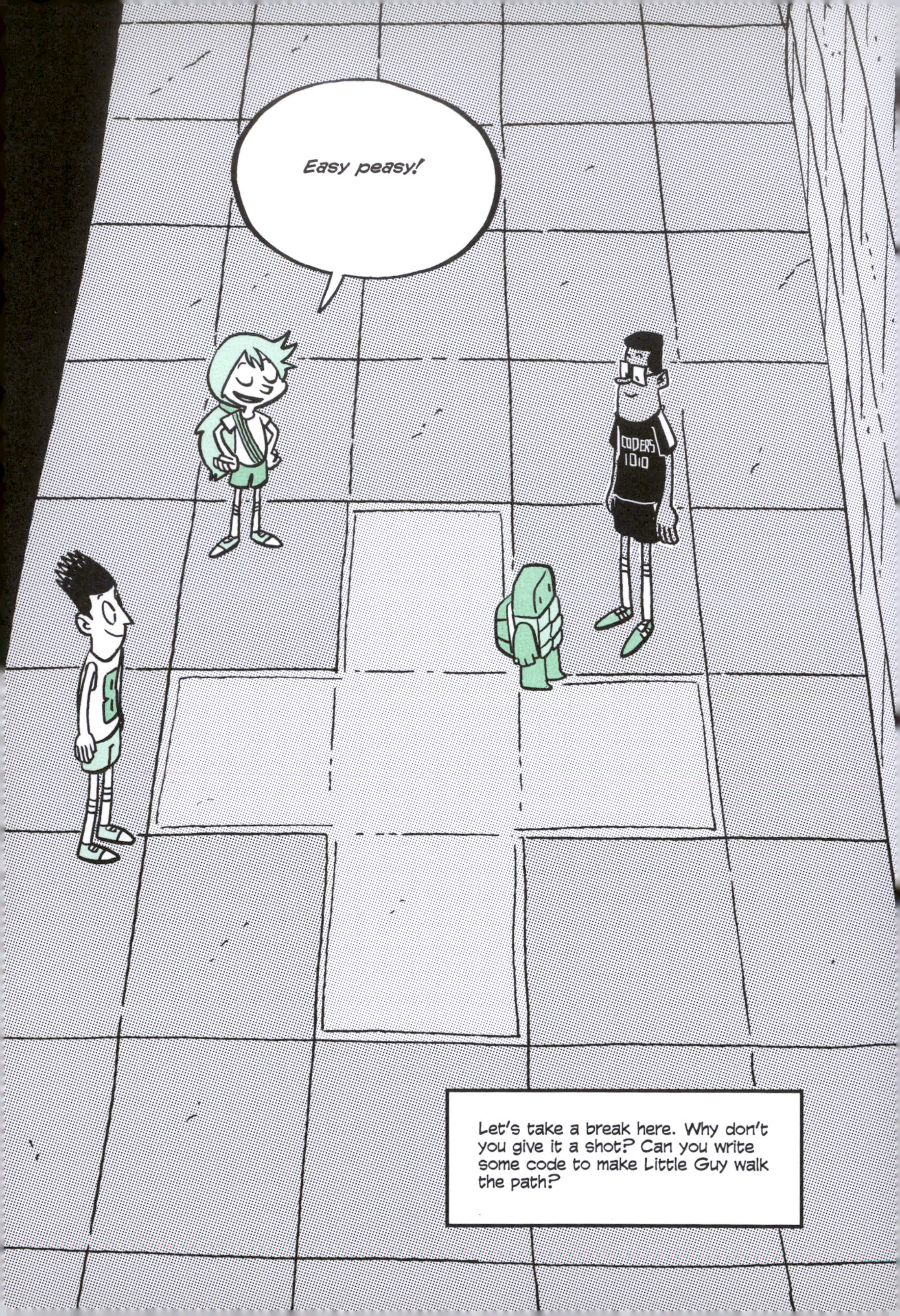
Easy peasy!
CODERS 1010
Let's take a break here. Why don't you give it a shot? Can you write some code to make Little Guy walk the path?

Chapter

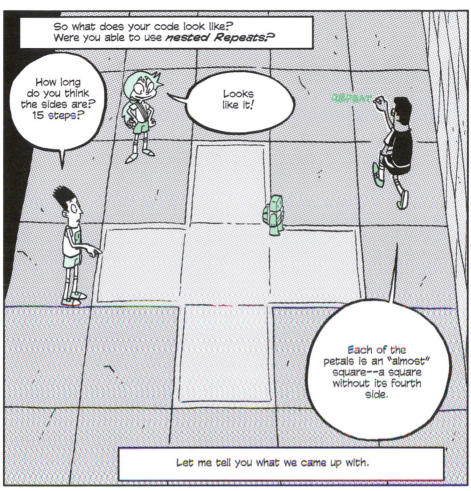

So what does your code look like? Were you able to use *nested Repeats?*

How long do you think the sides are? 15 steps?

Looks like it!

Each of the petals is an "almost" square—a square without its fourth side.

Let me tell you what we came up with.

So let's take code that draws a square—

```
REPEAT 4 [
FORWARD 15
RIGHT 90

]
```

--and change it to draw *three* sides instead of *four*.

```
REPEAT 3 [
FORWARD 15
RIGHT 90

]
```

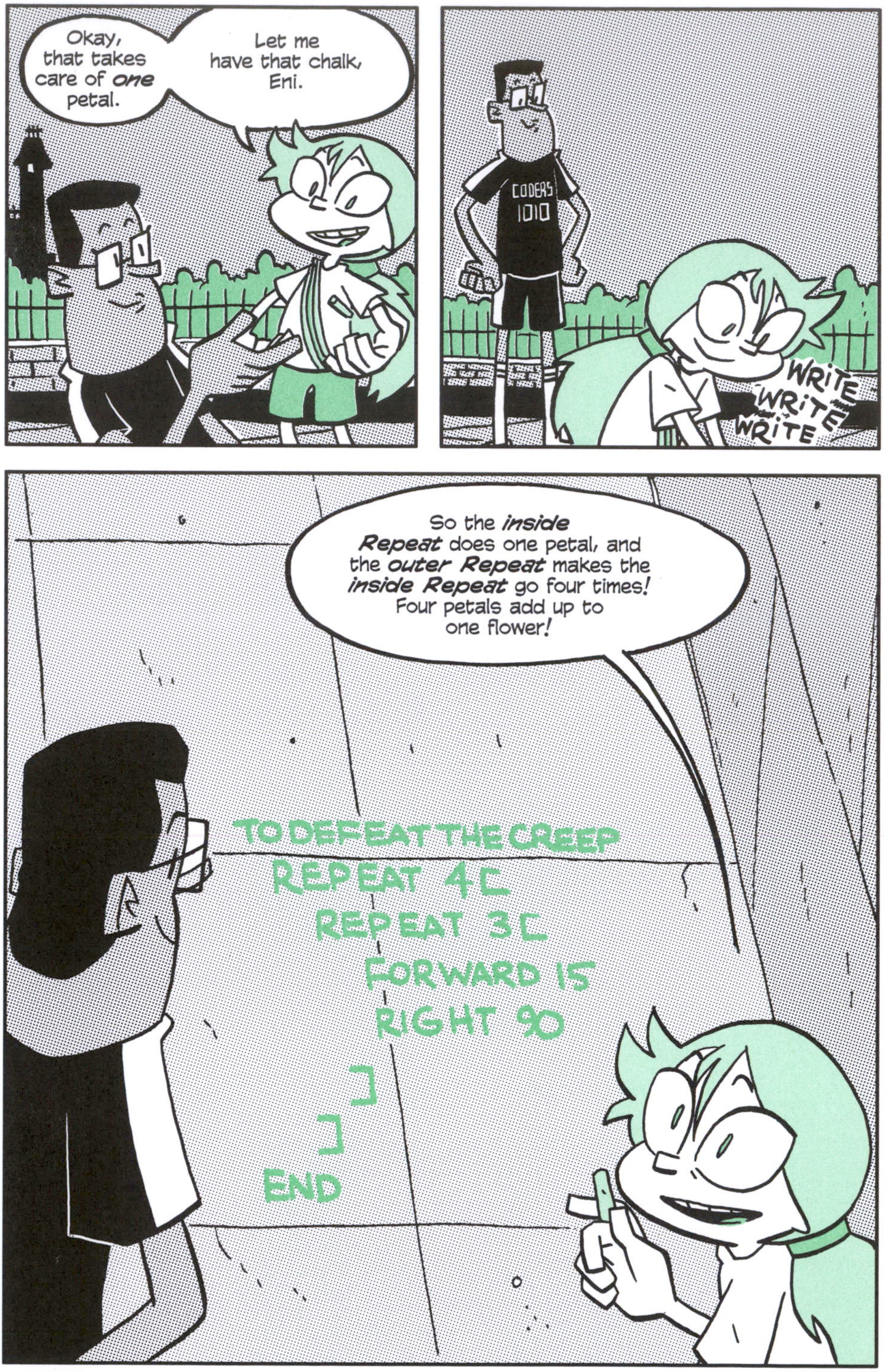
Okay, that takes care of *one* petal.
Let me have that chalk, Eni.
CODERS 1010
WRITE WRITE WRITE
So the *inside Repeat* does one petal, and the *outer Repeat* makes the *inside Repeat* go four times! Four petals add up to one flower!
TO DEFEAT THE CREEP
REPEAT 4 [
REPEAT 3 [
FORWARD 15
RIGHT 90
]
]
END

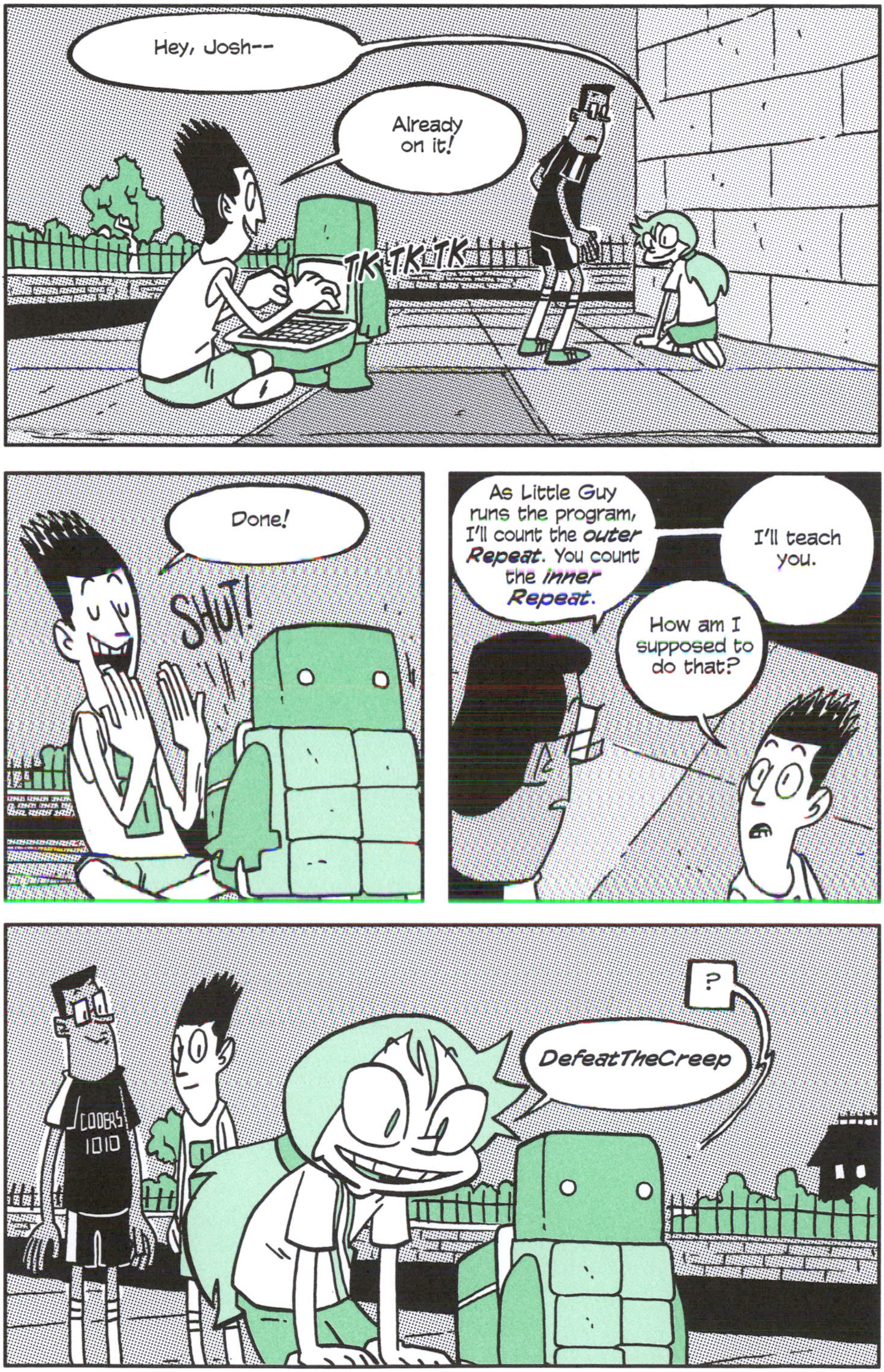
Hey, Josh--
Already on it!
TK TK TK
Done!
SHUT!
As Little Guy runs the program, I'll count the *outer Repeat*. You count the *inner Repeat*.
I'll teach you.
How am I supposed to do that?
CODERS 1010
?
DefeatTheCreep

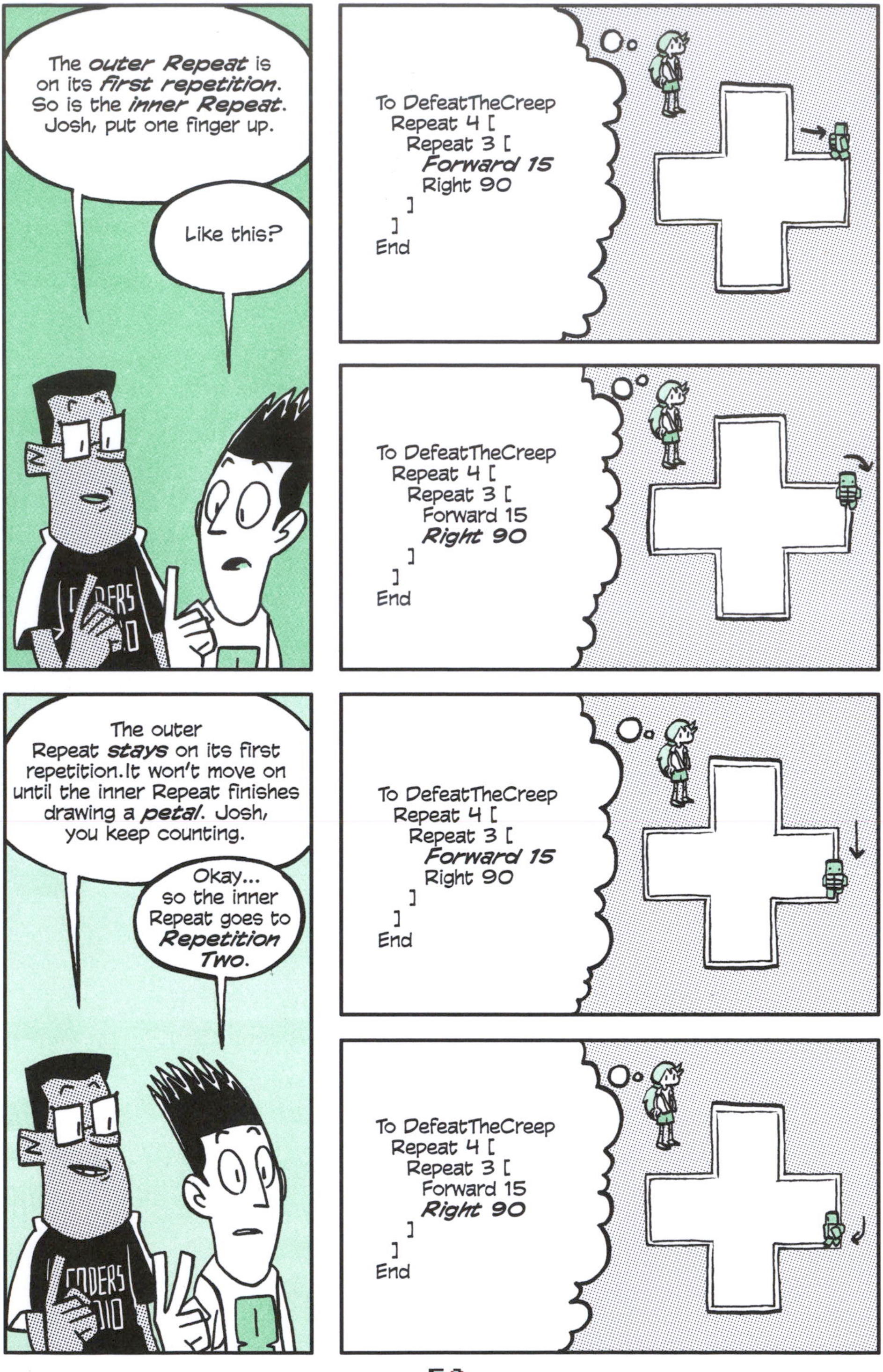
The *outer Repeat* is on its *first repetition*. So is the *inner Repeat*. Josh, put one finger up.
Like this?
To DefeatTheCreep
Repeat 4 [
Repeat 3 [
Forward 15
Right 90
]
]
End
To DefeatTheCreep
Repeat 4 [
Repeat 3 [
Forward 15
Right 90
]
]
End
The outer Repeat *stays* on its first repetition. It won't move on until the inner Repeat finishes drawing a *petal*. Josh, you keep counting.
Okay... so the inner Repeat goes to *Repetition Two*.
To DefeatTheCreep
Repeat 4 [
Repeat 3 [
Forward 15
Right 90
]
]
End
To DefeatTheCreep
Repeat 4 [
Repeat 3 [
Forward 15
Right 90
]
]
End

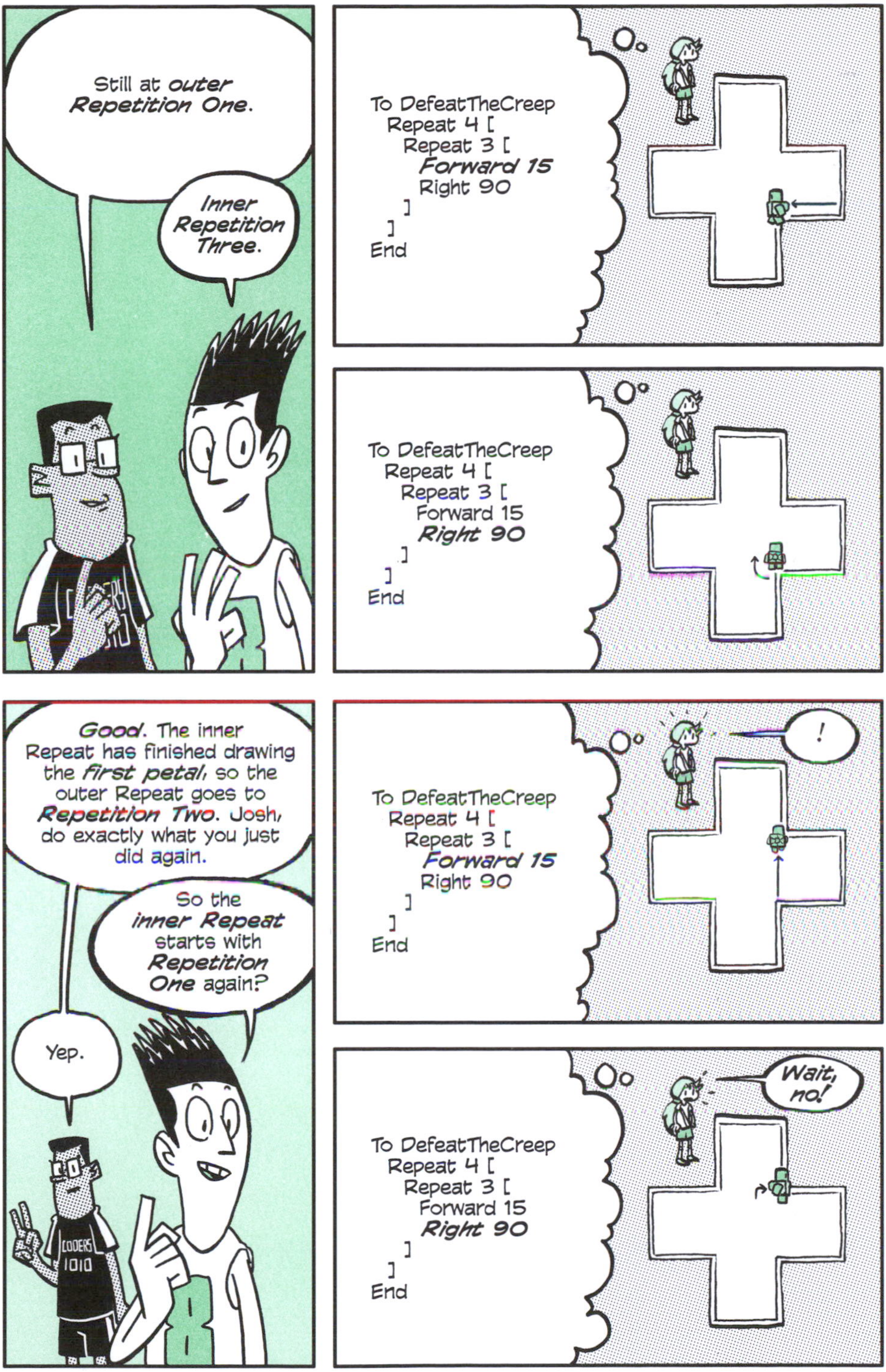

Still at *outer* *Repetition One*.
Inner Repetition Three.
To DefeatTheCreep
Repeat 4 [
Repeat 3 [
Forward 15
Right 90
]
]
End
To DefeatTheCreep
Repeat 4 [
Repeat 3 [
Forward 15
Right 90
]
]
End
Good. The inner Repeat has finished drawing the *first petal*, so the outer Repeat goes to *Repetition Two*. Josh, do exactly what you just did again.
So the *inner Repeat* starts with *Repetition One* again?
Yep.
CODERS 1010
To DefeatTheCreep
Repeat 4 [
Repeat 3 [
Forward 15
Right 90
]
]
End
!
To DefeatTheCreep
Repeat 4 [
Repeat 3 [
Forward 15
Right 90
]
]
End
Wait, no!

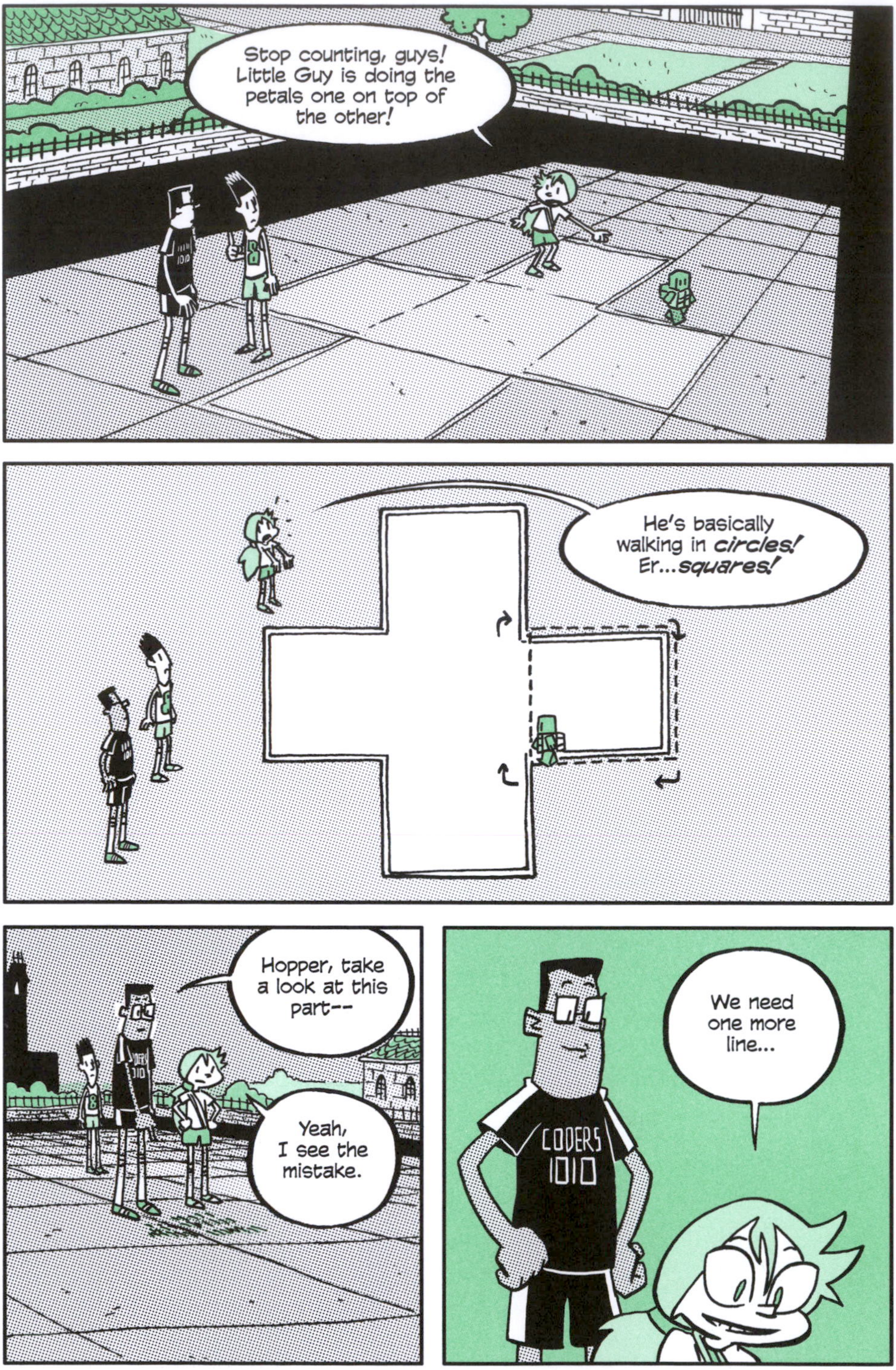
Stop counting, guys! Little Guy is doing the petals one on top of the other!
He's basically walking in *circles!* Er...*squares!*
Hopper, take a look at this part--
Yeah, I see the mistake.
CODERS 1010
We need one more line...

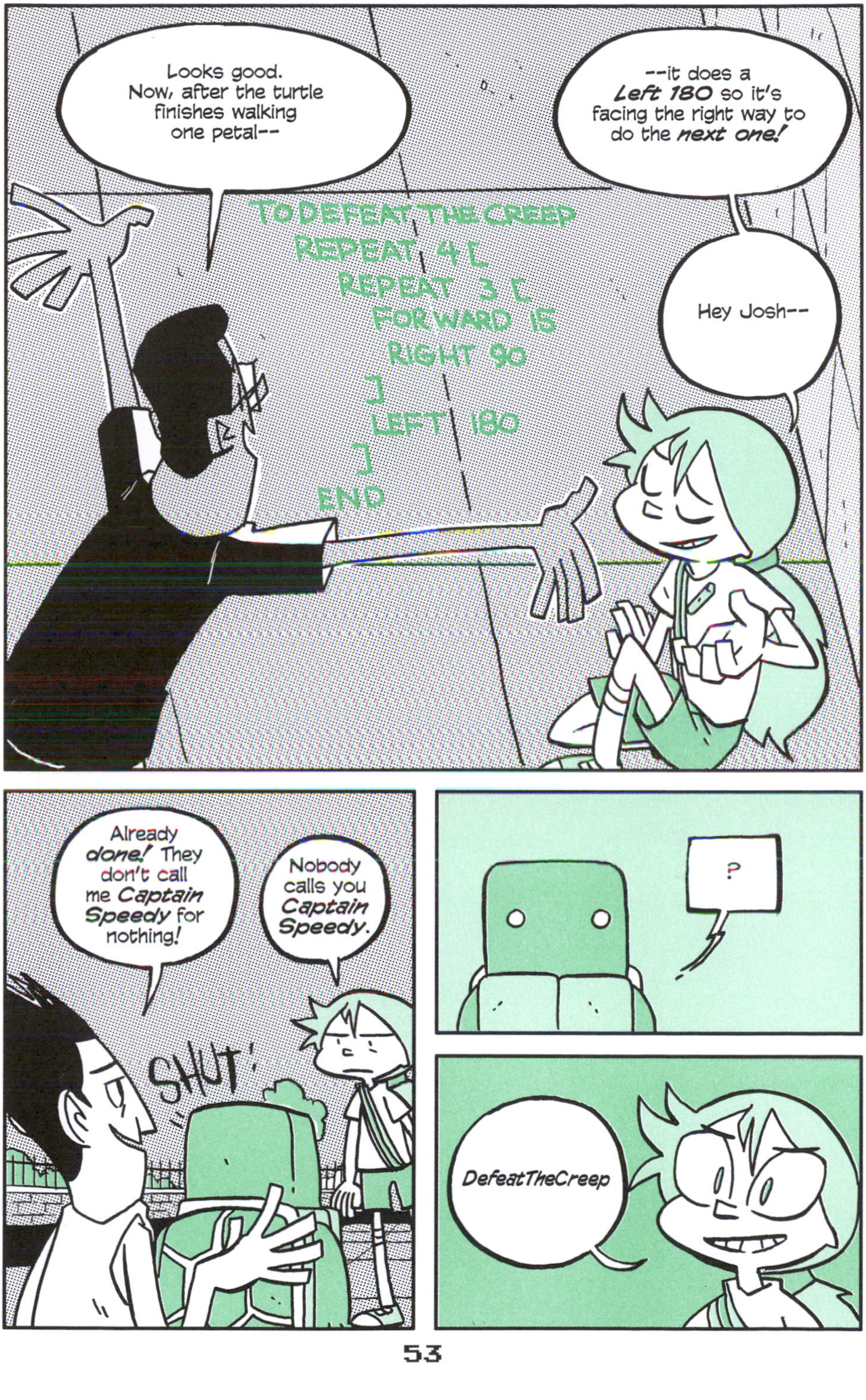
Looks good. Now, after the turtle finishes walking one petal--
--it does a *Left 180* so it's facing the right way to do the *next one!*
TO DEFEAT THE CREEP
REPEAT 4 [
REPEAT 3 [
FORWARD 15
RIGHT 90
]
LEFT 180
]
END
Hey Josh--
Already *done!* They don't call me *Captain Speedy* for nothing!
Nobody calls you *Captain Speedy.*
SHUT!
?
DefeatTheCreep

Outer One.

Inner Three.

```
To DefeatTheCreep
  Repeat 4 [
    Repeat 3 [
      Forward 15
      Right 90
    ]

    Left 180
  ]
End
```

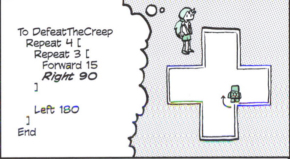

```
To DefeatTheCreep
  Repeat 4 [
    Repeat 3 [
      Forward 15
      Right 90
    ]

    Left 180
  ]
End
```

The inner Repeat has finished all three of its repetitions, but Little Guy still has one more instruction to follow.

What do I do now?

Just wait.

Let's see if our fix worked!

```
To DefeatTheCreep
  Repeat 4 [
    Repeat 3 [
      Forward 15
      Right 90
    ]

    Left 180
  ]
End
```

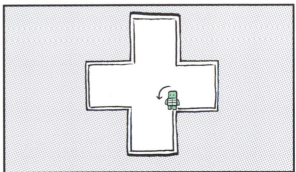

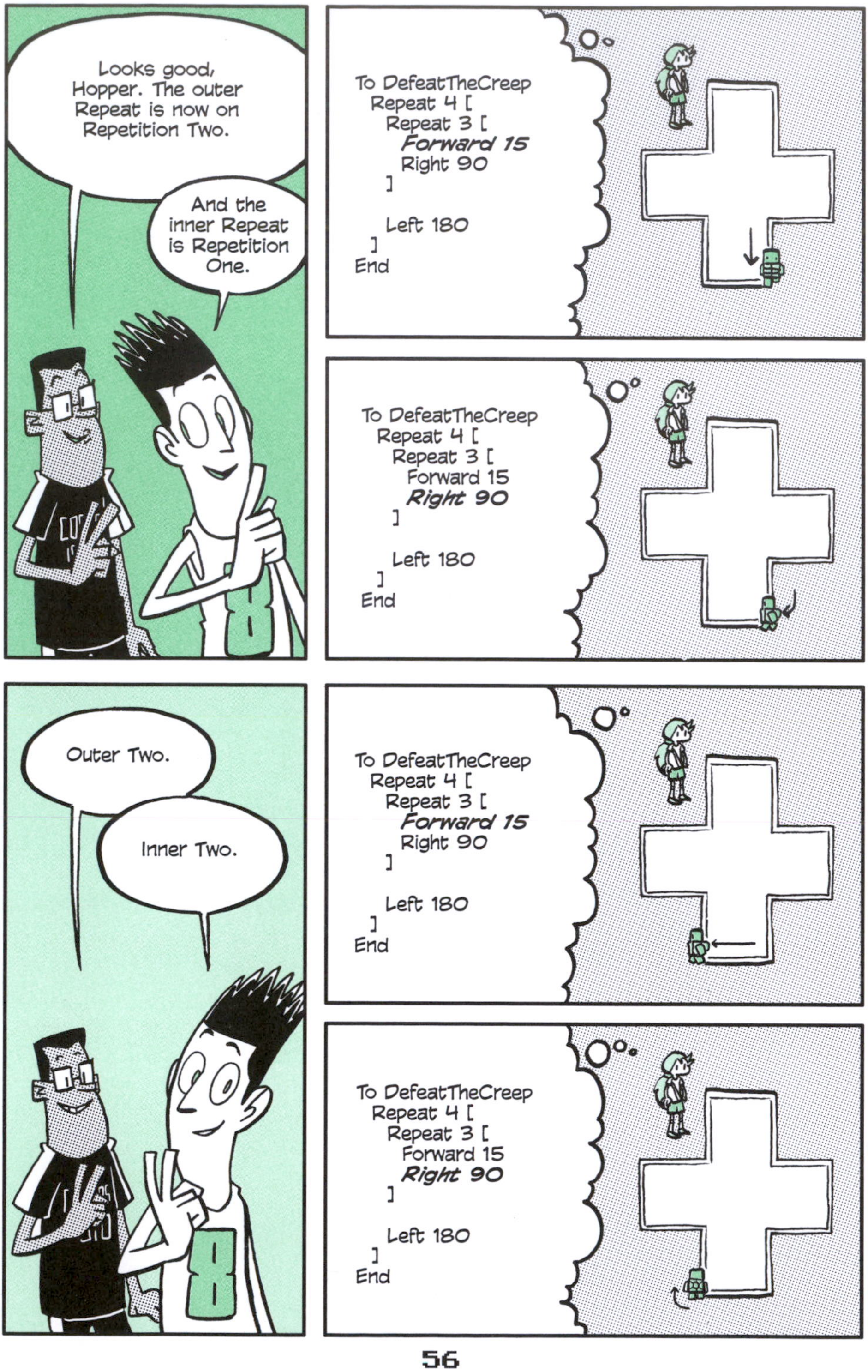
Looks good, Hopper. The outer Repeat is now on Repetition Two.
And the inner Repeat is Repetition One.
To DefeatTheCreep
Repeat 4 [
Repeat 3 [
Forward 15
Right 90
]
Left 180
]
End
To DefeatTheCreep
Repeat 4 [
Repeat 3 [
Forward 15
Right 90
]
Left 180
]
End
Outer Two.
Inner Two.
To DefeatTheCreep
Repeat 4 [
Repeat 3 [
Forward 15
Right 90
]
Left 180
]
End
To DefeatTheCreep
Repeat 4 [
Repeat 3 [
Forward 15
Right 90
]
Left 180
]
End

Outer Two.

Inner Three.

```
To DefeatTheCreep
  Repeat 4 [
    Repeat 3 [
      Forward 15
      Right 90
    ]

    Left 180
  ]
End
```

```
To DefeatTheCreep
  Repeat 4 [
    Repeat 3 [
      Forward 15
      Right 90
    ]

    Left 180
  ]
End
```

Here's the part where I wait again?

Yep.

Little Guy did the second petal *perfectly!*

```
To DefeatTheCreep
  Repeat 4 [
    Repeat 3 [
      Forward 15
      Right 90
    ]

    Left 180
  ]
End
```

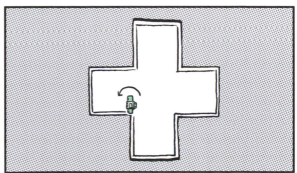

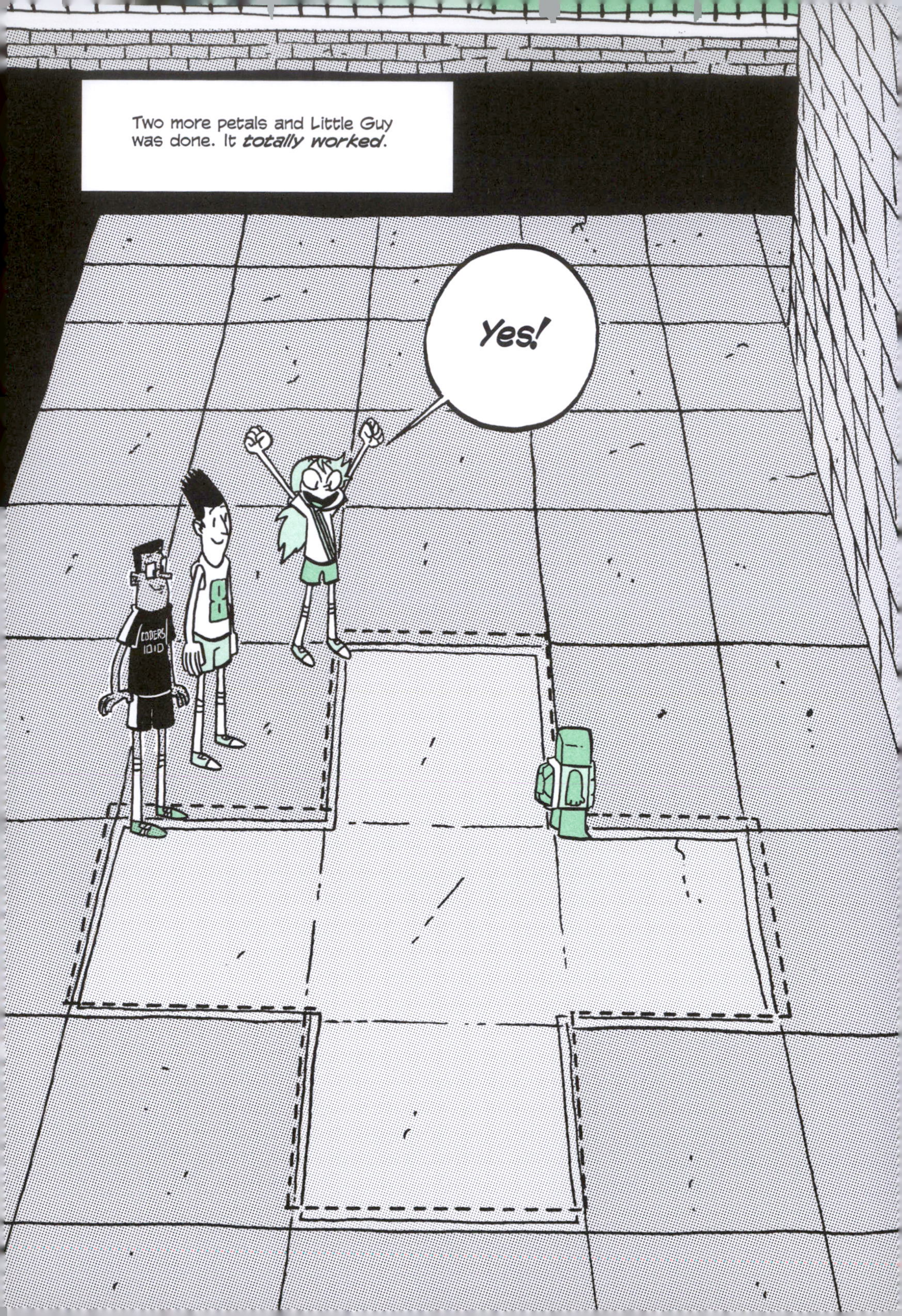
Two more petals and Little Guy was done. It *totally worked*.
Yes!

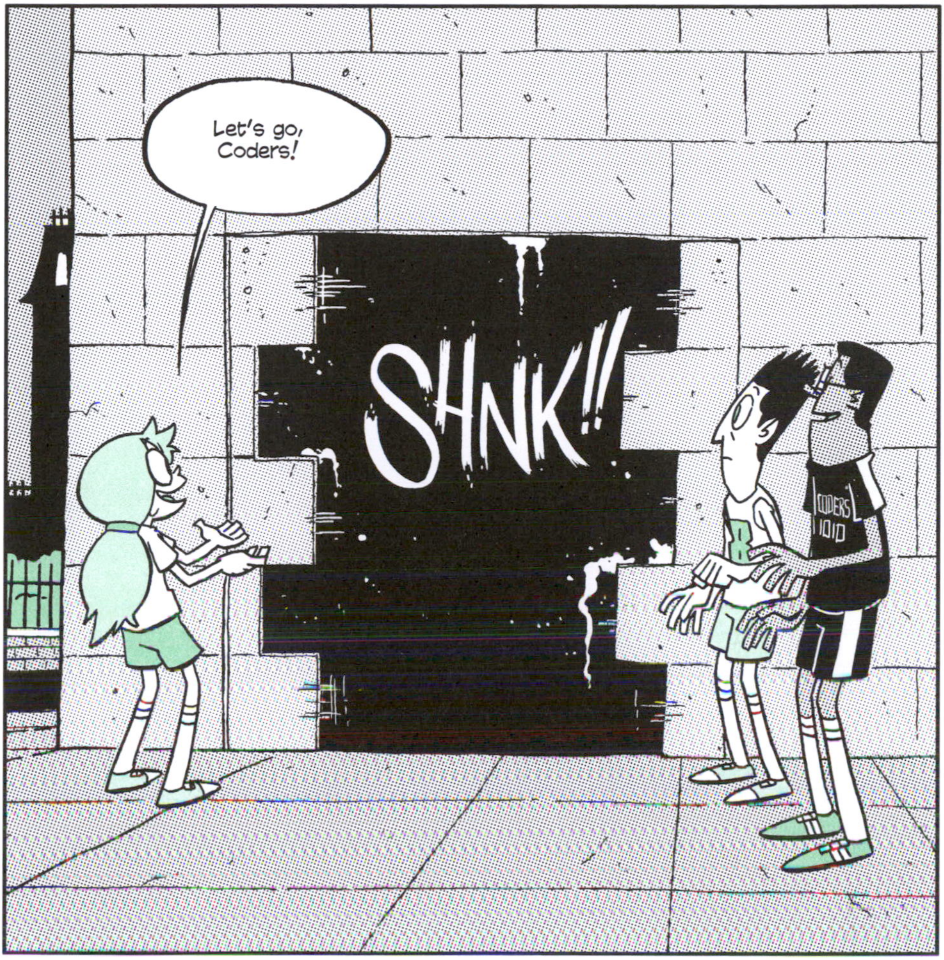
Let's go, Coders!
SHNK!!
CODERS 1010

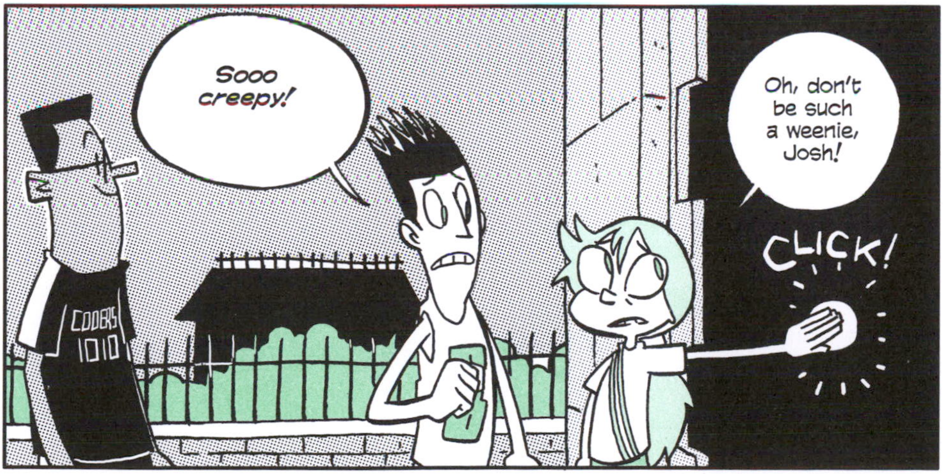
Sooo creepy!
Oh, don't be such a weenie, Josh!
CLICK!
CODERS 1010

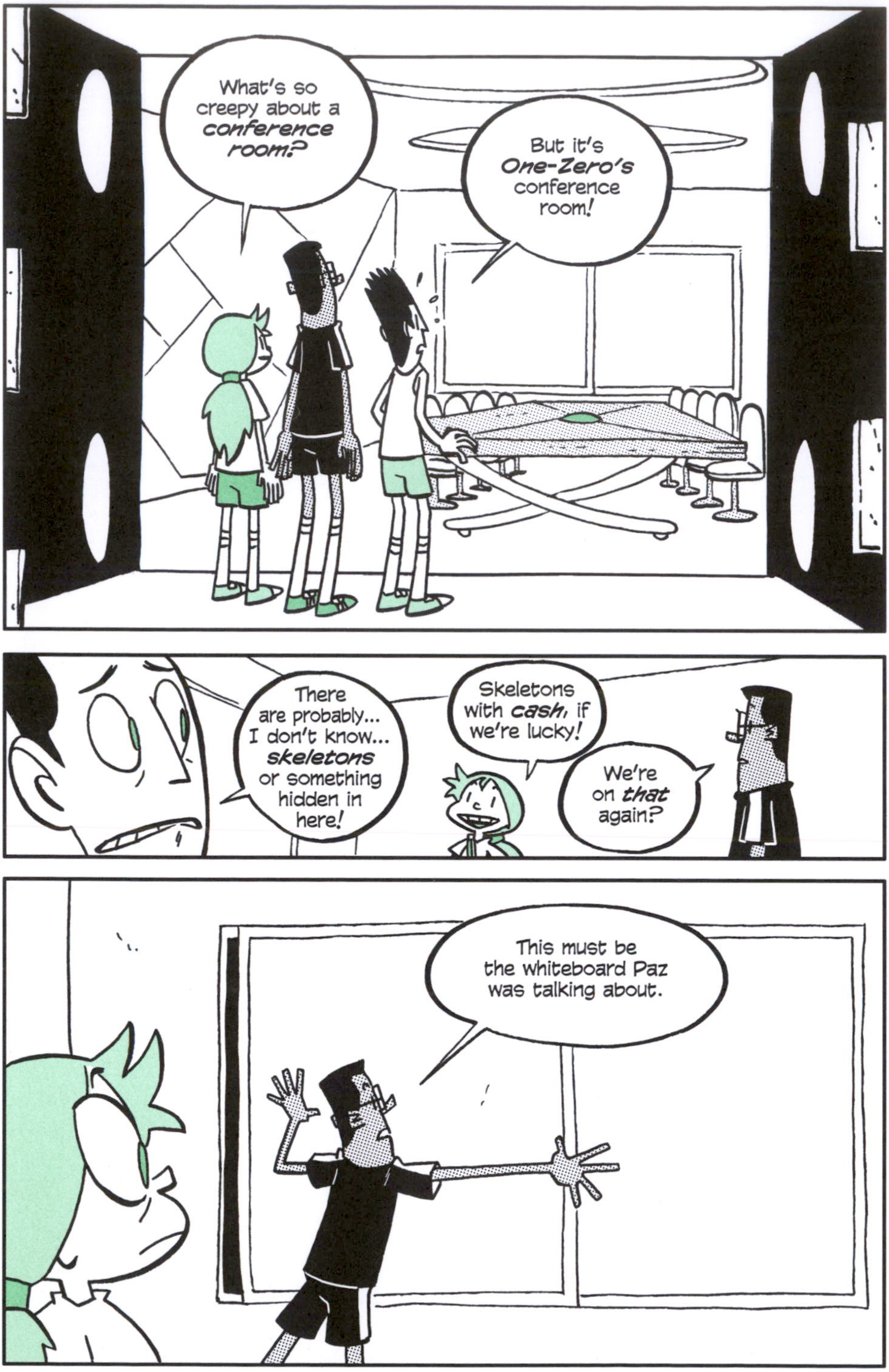
What's so creepy about a *conference room?*
But it's *One-Zero's* conference room!
There are probably... I don't know... *skeletons* or something hidden in here!
Skeletons with *cash*, if we're lucky!
We're on *that* again?
This must be the whiteboard Paz was talking about.

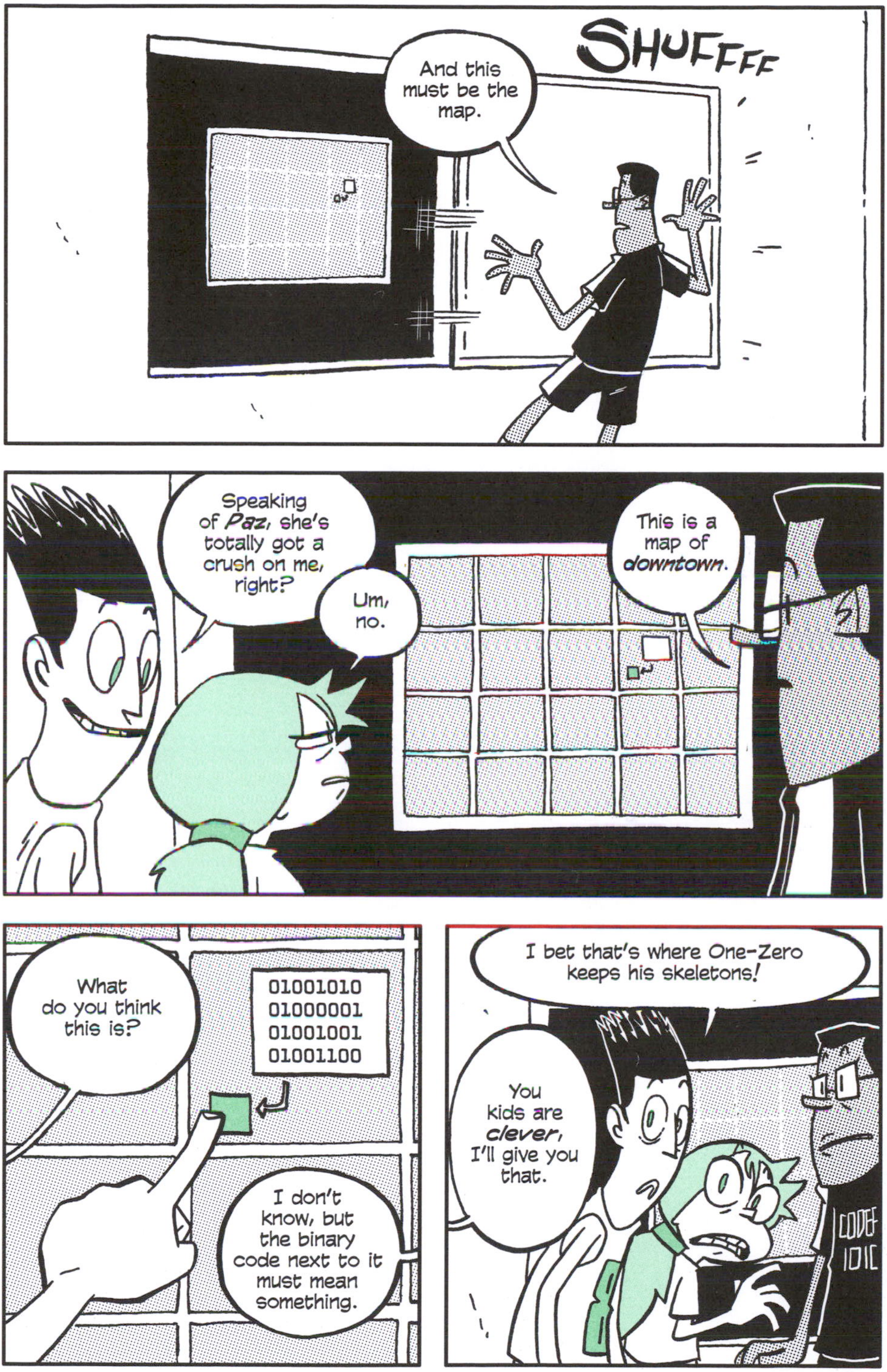

SHUFFFF
And this must be the map.
Speaking of *Paz*, she's totally got a crush on me, right?
Um, no.
This is a map of *downtown*.
What do you think this is?
01001010
01000001
01001001
01001100
I don't know, but the binary code next to it must mean something.
I bet that's where One-Zero keeps his skeletons!
You kids are *clever*, I'll give you that.
CODE
1010

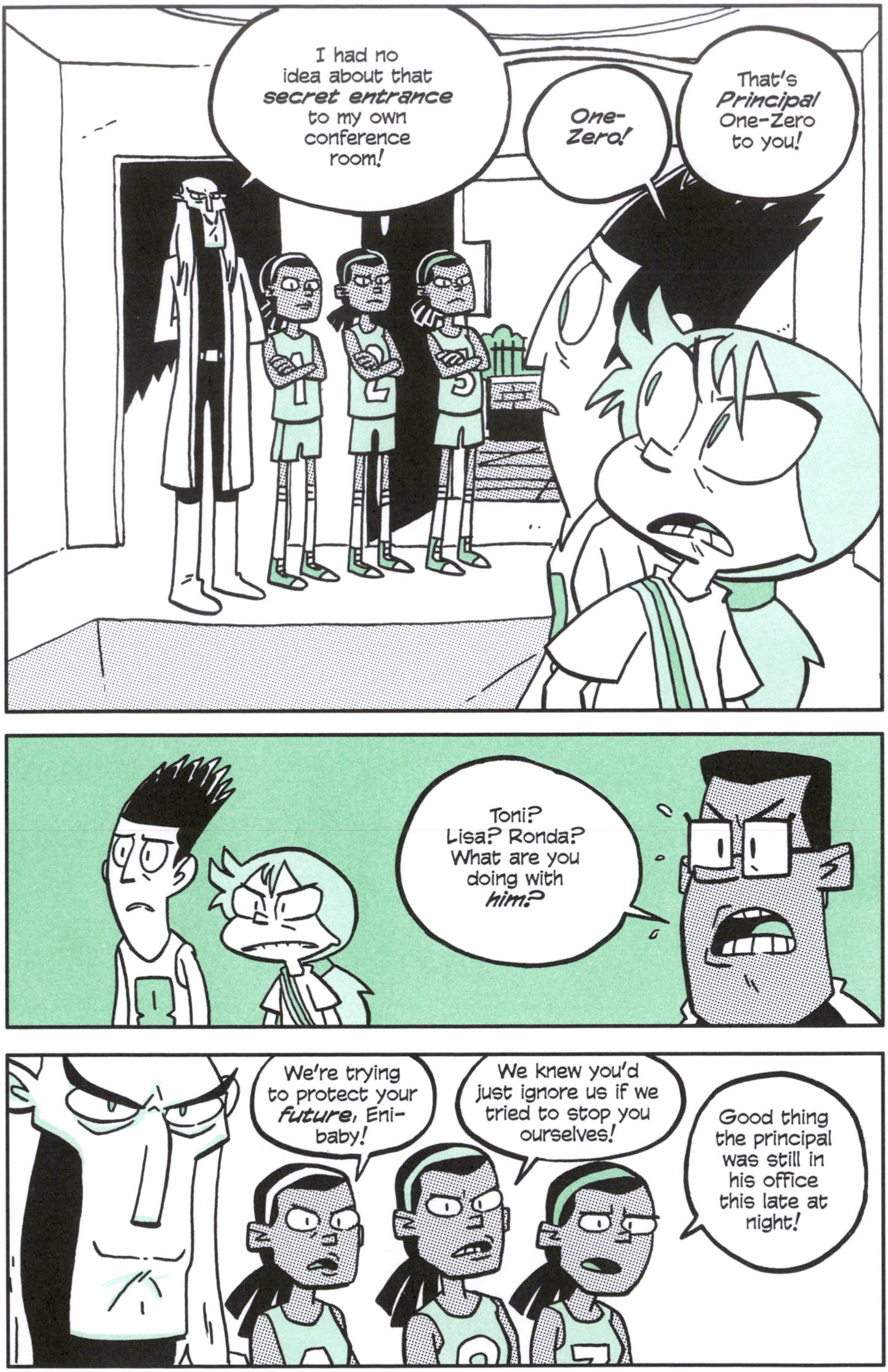
I had no idea about that ***secret entrance*** to my own conference room!
One-Zero!
That's ***Principal*** One-Zero to you!
Toni? Lisa? Ronda? What are you doing with ***him?***
We're trying to protect your ***future***, Eni-baby!
We knew you'd just ignore us if we tried to stop you ourselves!
Good thing the principal was still in his office this late at night!

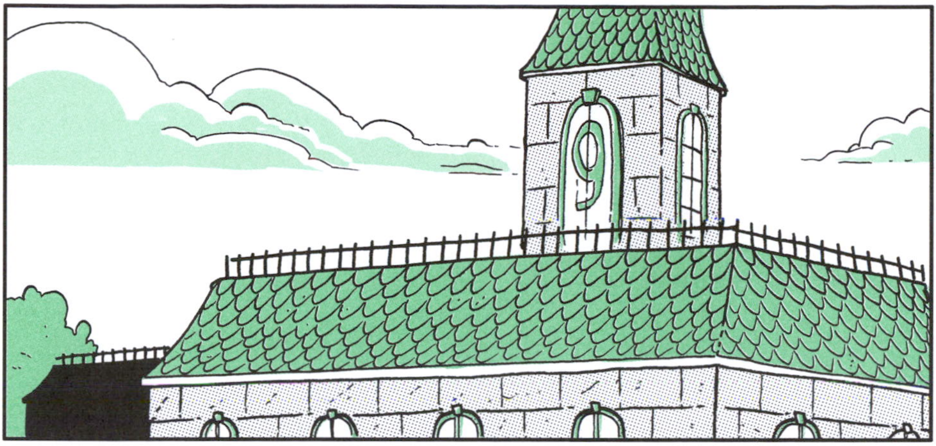

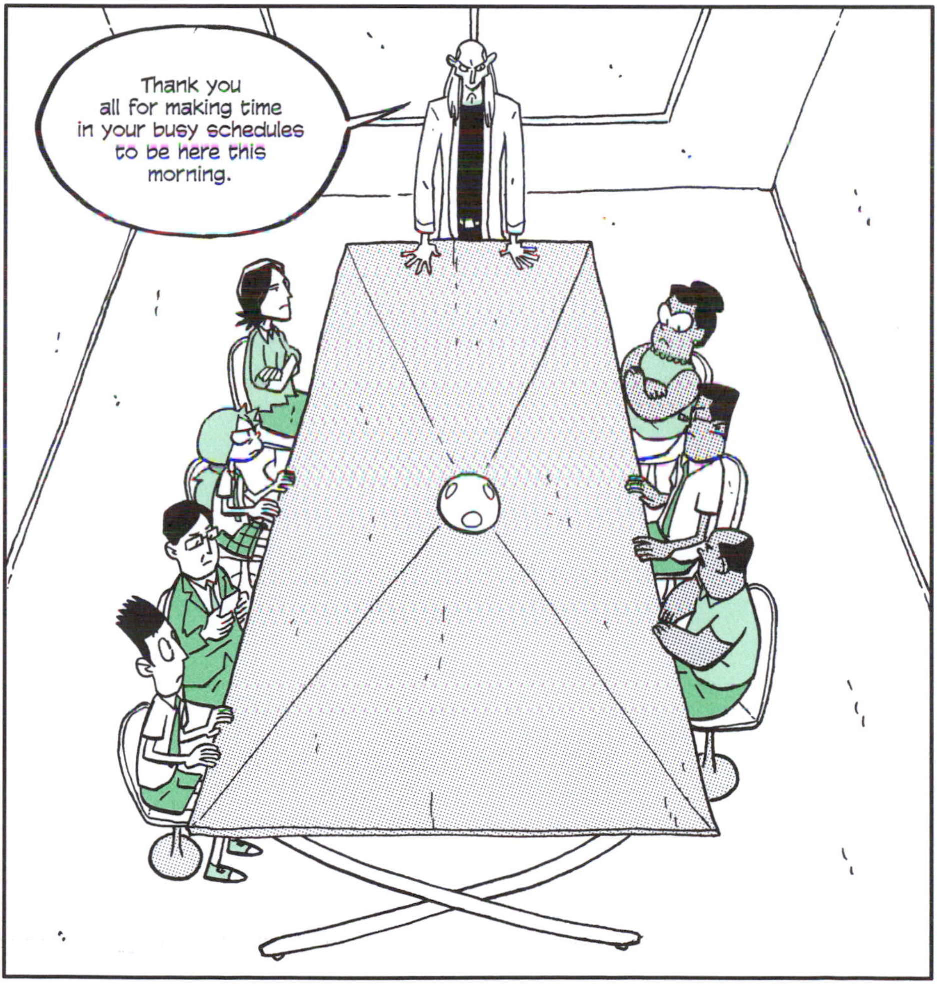
Thank you all for making time in your busy schedules to be here this morning.

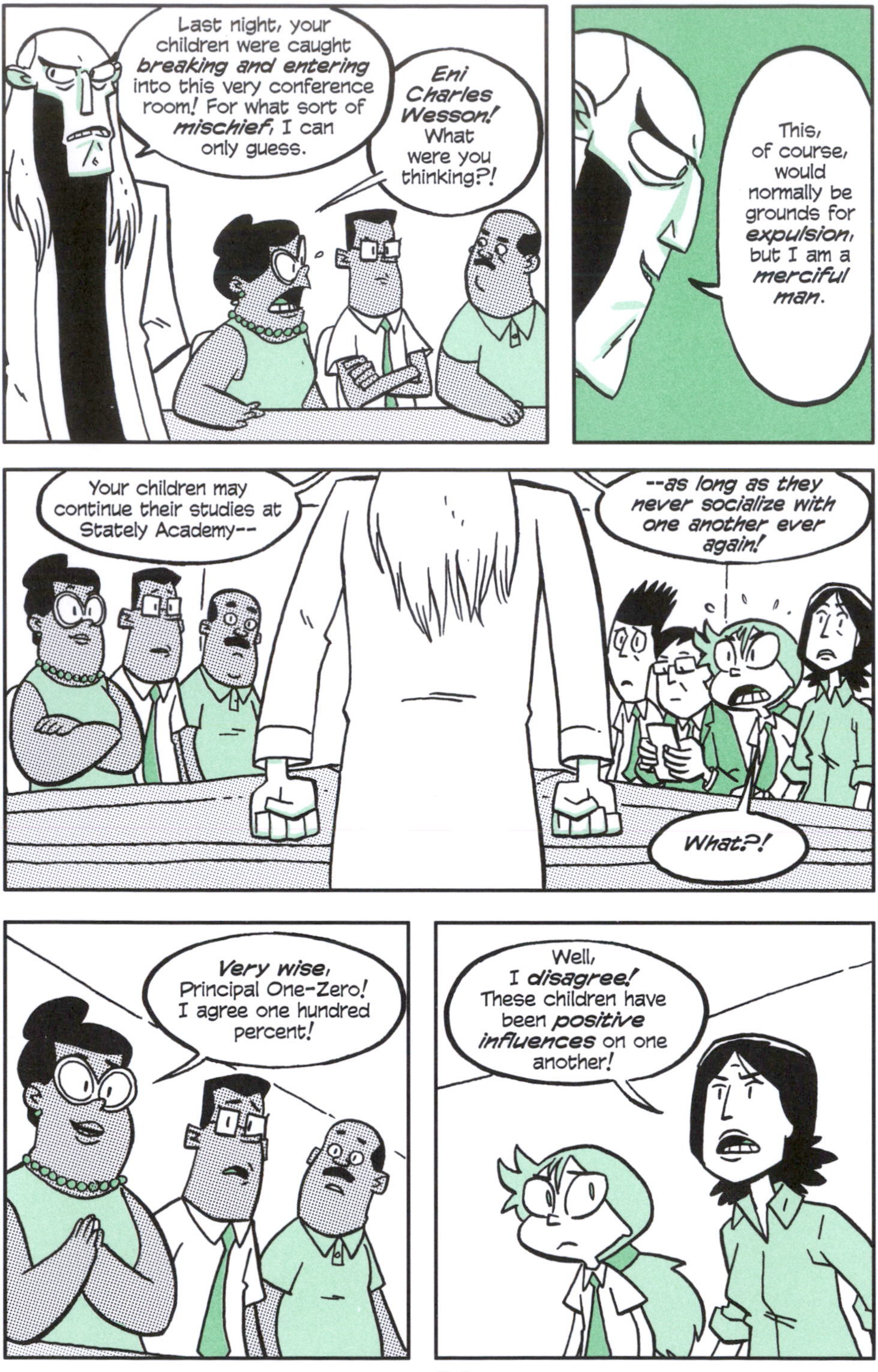

Last night, your children were caught *breaking and entering* into this very conference room! For what sort of *mischief*, I can only guess.
Eni Charles Wesson! What were you thinking?!
This, of course, would normally be grounds for *expulsion*, but I am a *merciful man*.
Your children may continue their studies at Stately Academy--
--as long as they never socialize with one another ever again!
What?!
Very wise, Principal One-Zero! I agree one hundred percent!
Well, I *disagree!* These children have been *positive influences* on one another!

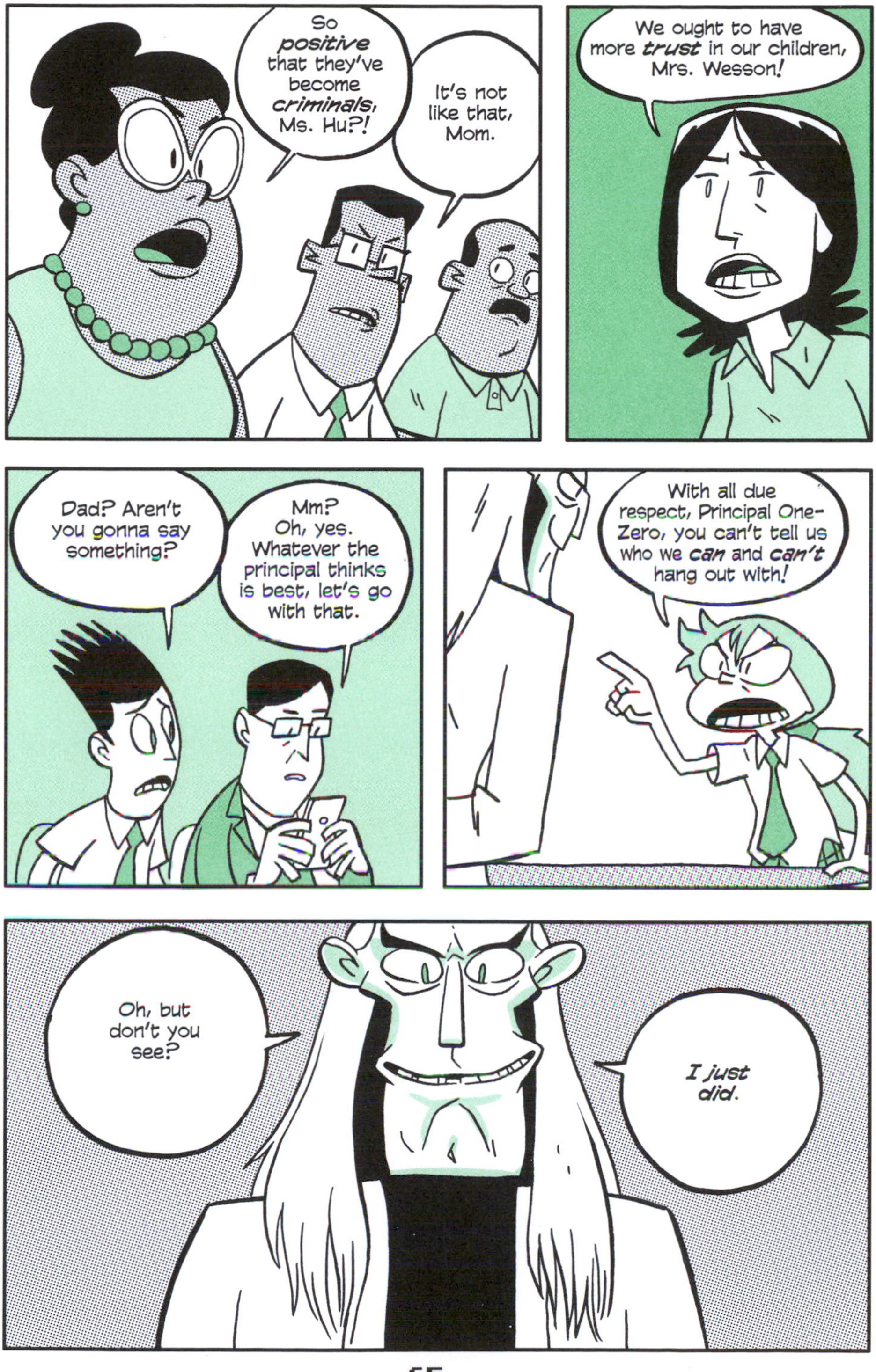

So *positive* that they've become *criminals*, Ms. Hu?!
It's not like that, Mom.
We ought to have more *trust* in our children, Mrs. Wesson!
Dad? Aren't you gonna say something?
Mm? Oh, yes. Whatever the principal thinks is best, let's go with that.
With all due respect, Principal One-Zero, you can't tell us who we *can* and *can't* hang out with!
Oh, but don't you see?
I just did.

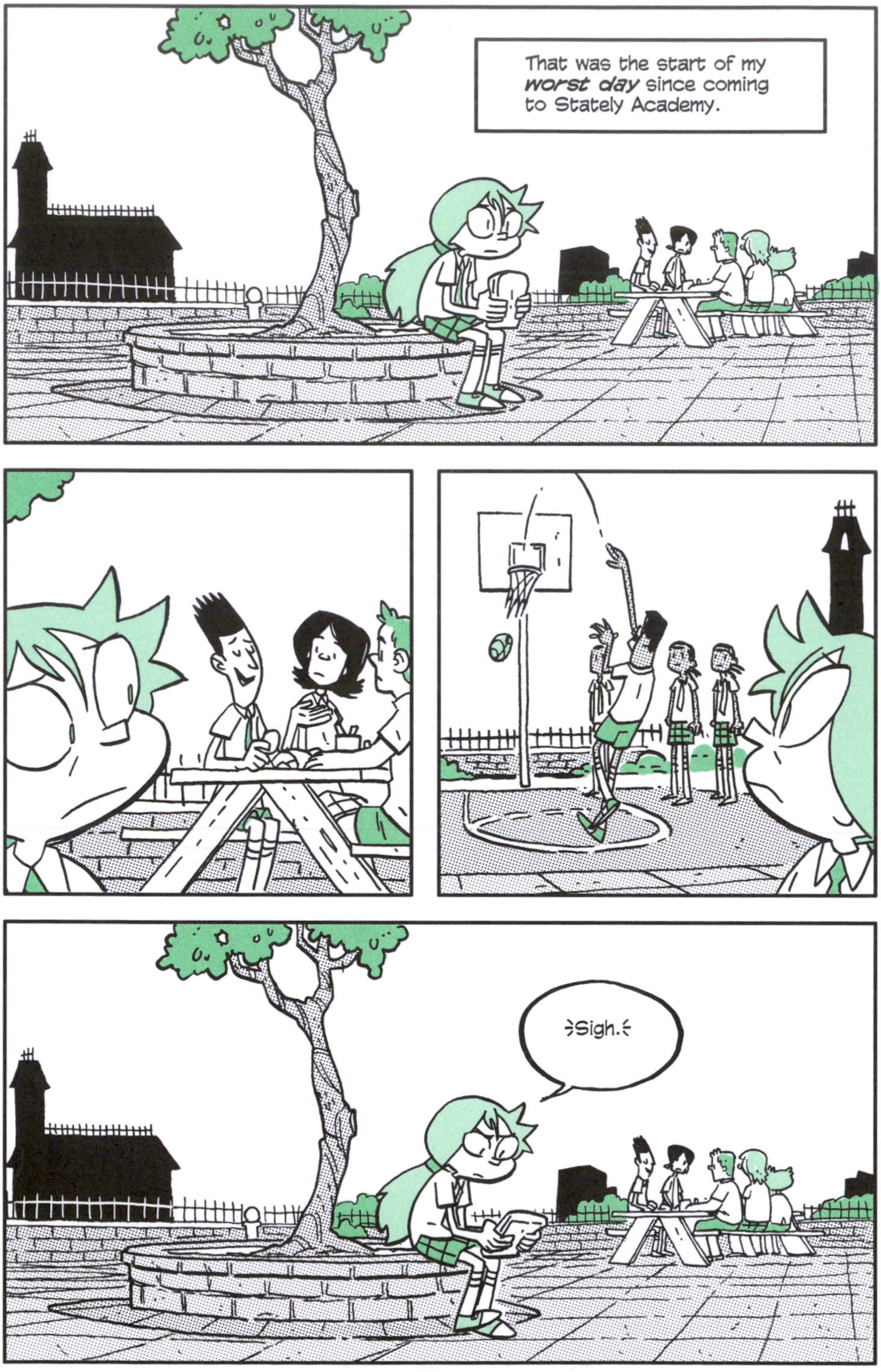
That was the start of my ***worst day*** since coming to Stately Academy.
Sigh.

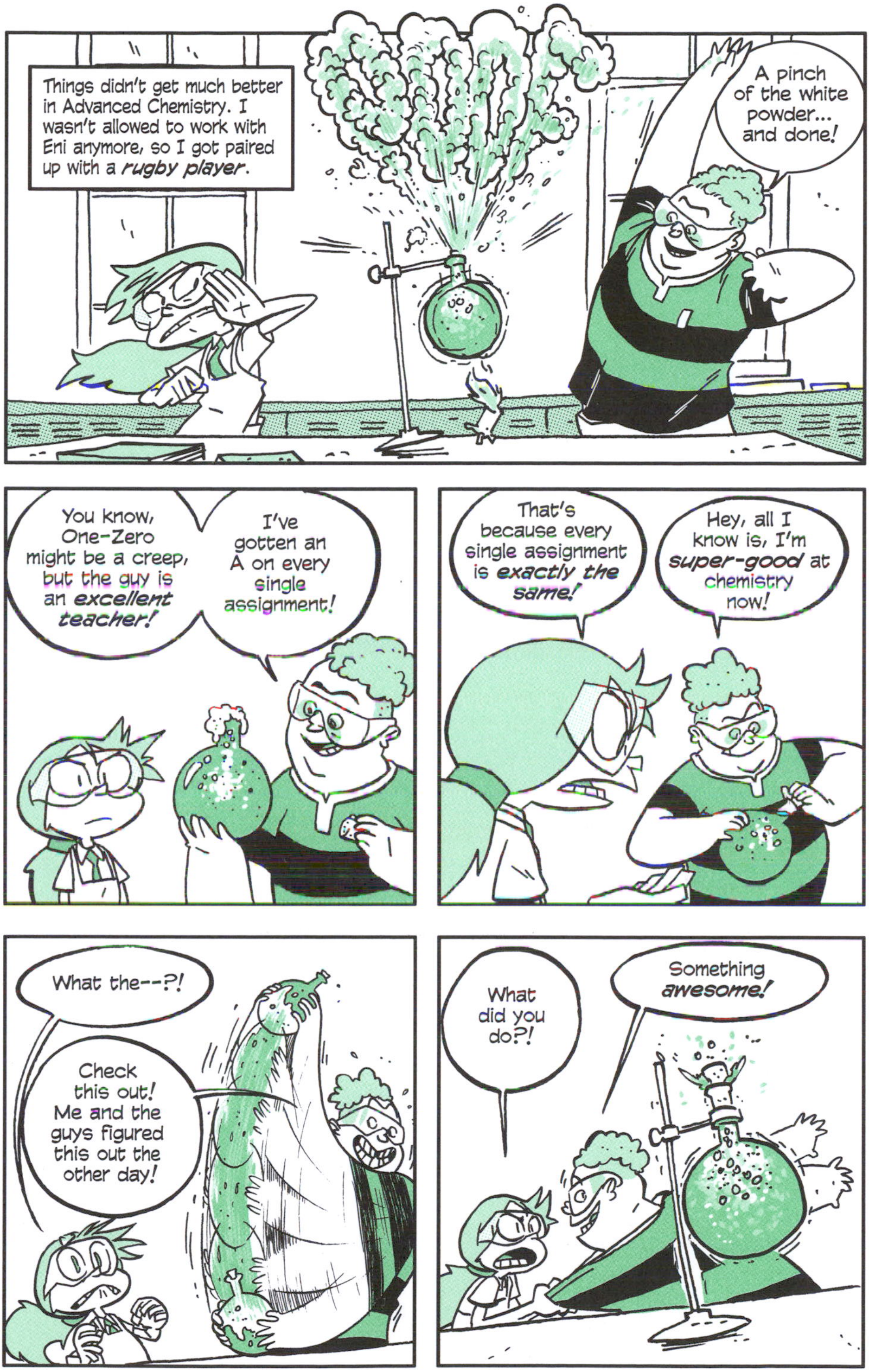
Things didn't get much better in Advanced Chemistry. I wasn't allowed to work with Eni anymore, so I got paired up with a *rugby player*.
A pinch of the white powder... and done!
You know, One-Zero might be a creep, but the guy is an *excellent teacher!*
I've gotten an A on every single assignment!
That's because every single assignment is *exactly the same!*
Hey, all I know is, I'm *super-good* at chemistry now!
What the--?!
Check this out! Me and the guys figured this out the other day!
What did you do?!
Something *awesome!*

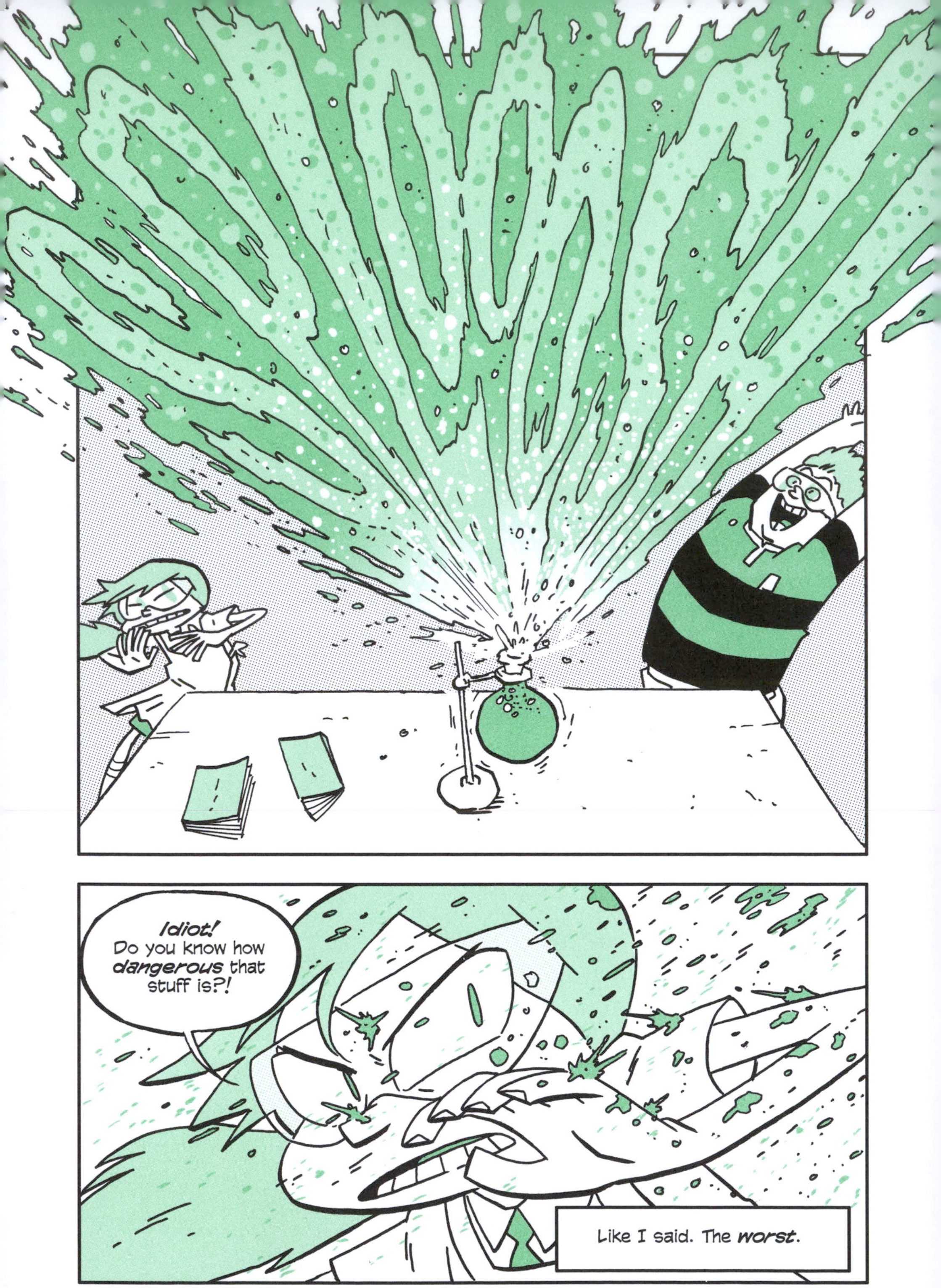
Idiot! Do you know how *dangerous* that stuff is?!
Like I said. The *worst*.

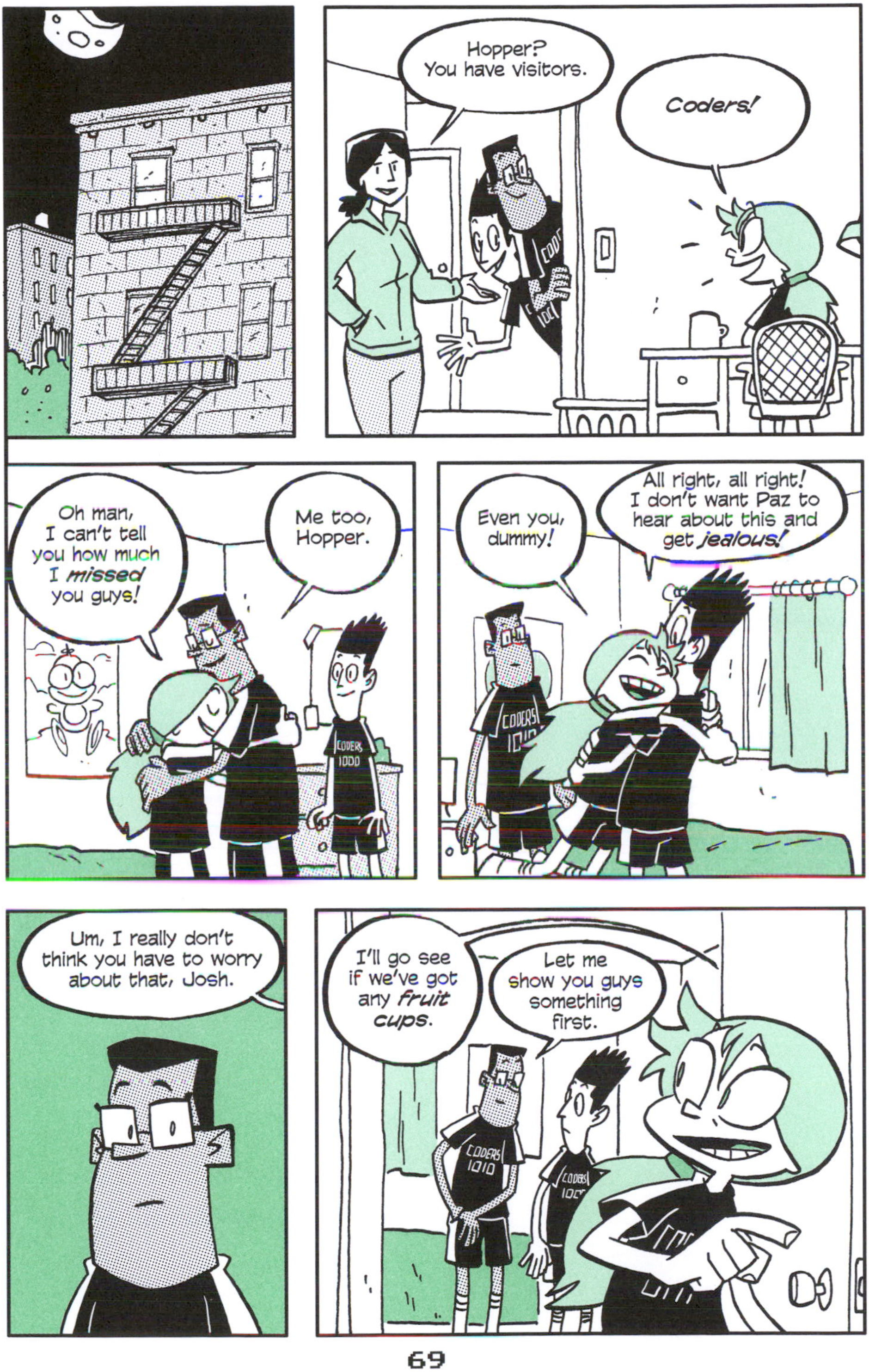
Hopper? You have visitors.
Coders!
Oh man, I can't tell you how much I *missed* you guys!
Me too, Hopper.
Even you, dummy!
All right, all right! I don't want Paz to hear about this and get *jealous!*
Um, I really don't think you have to worry about that, Josh.
I'll go see if we've got any *fruit cups*.
Let me show you guys something first.

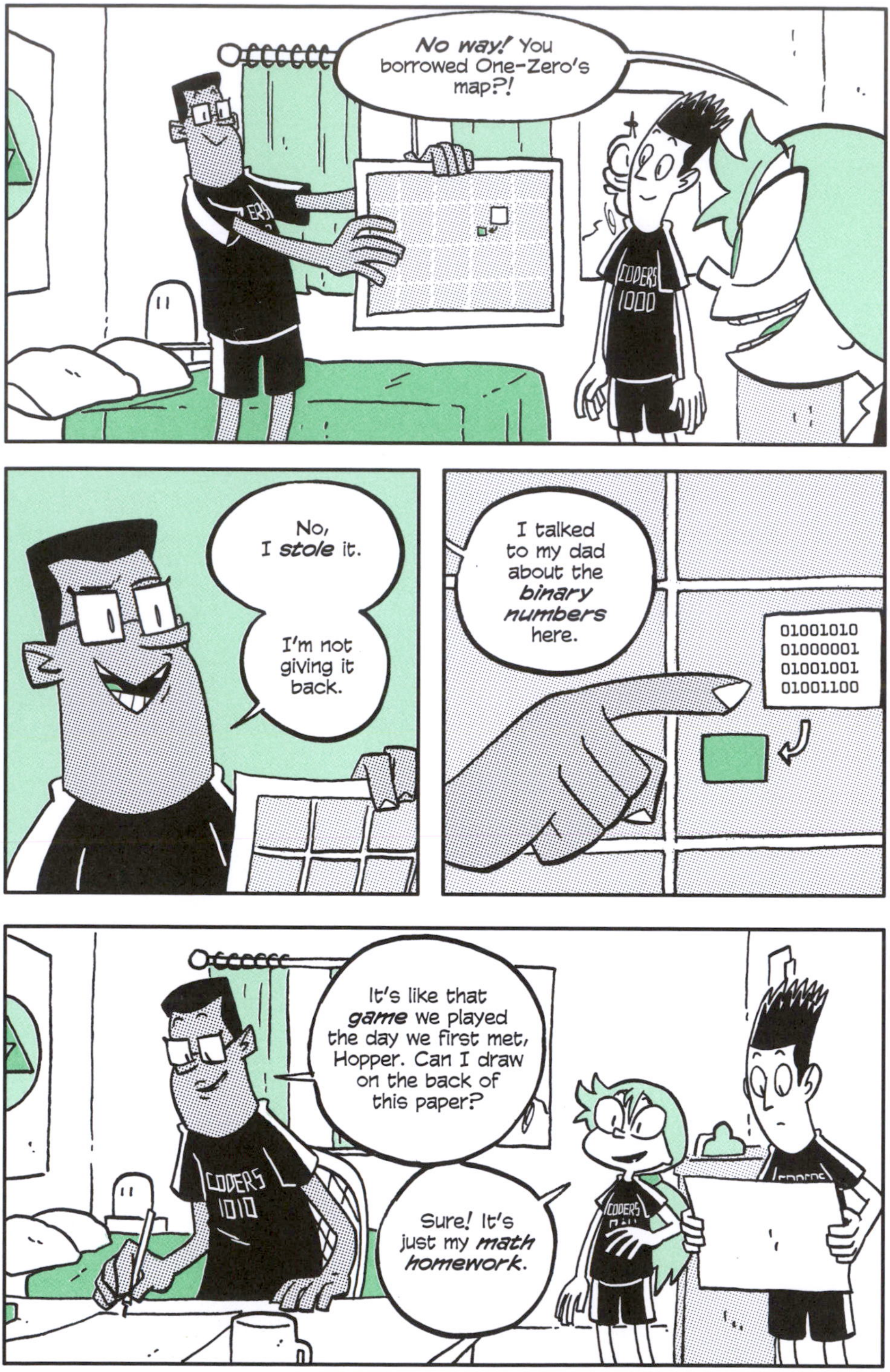
No way! You borrowed One-Zero's map?!
No, I stole it.
I'm not giving it back.
I talked to my dad about the binary numbers here.
01001010
01000001
01001001
01001100
It's like that game we played the day we first met, Hopper. Can I draw on the back of this paper?
Sure! It's just my math homework.

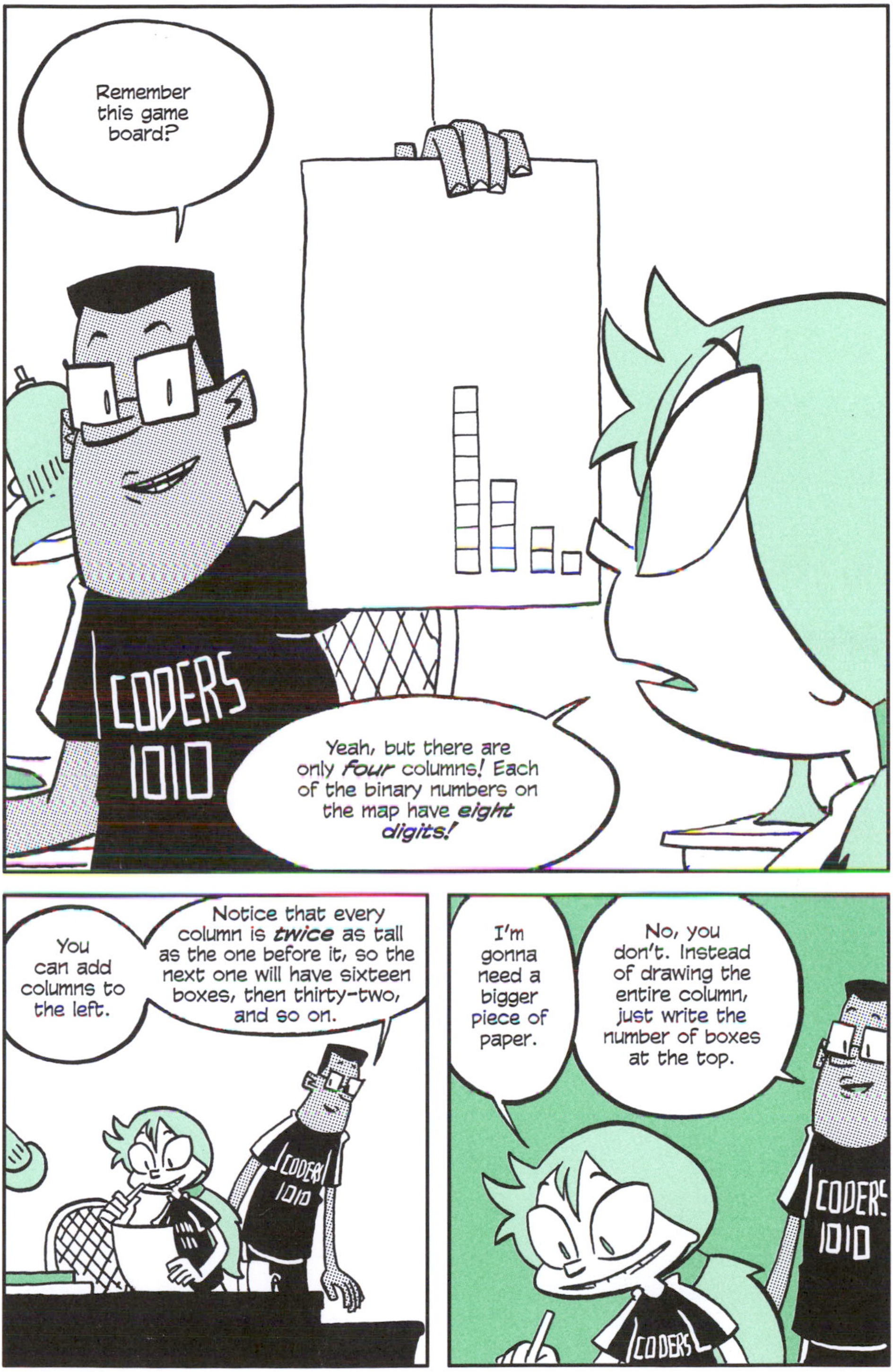

Remember this game board?
Yeah, but there are only *four* columns! Each of the binary numbers on the map have *eight digits!*
You can add columns to the left.
Notice that every column is *twice* as tall as the one before it, so the next one will have sixteen boxes, then thirty-two, and so on.
I'm gonna need a bigger piece of paper.
No, you don't. Instead of drawing the entire column, just write the number of boxes at the top.

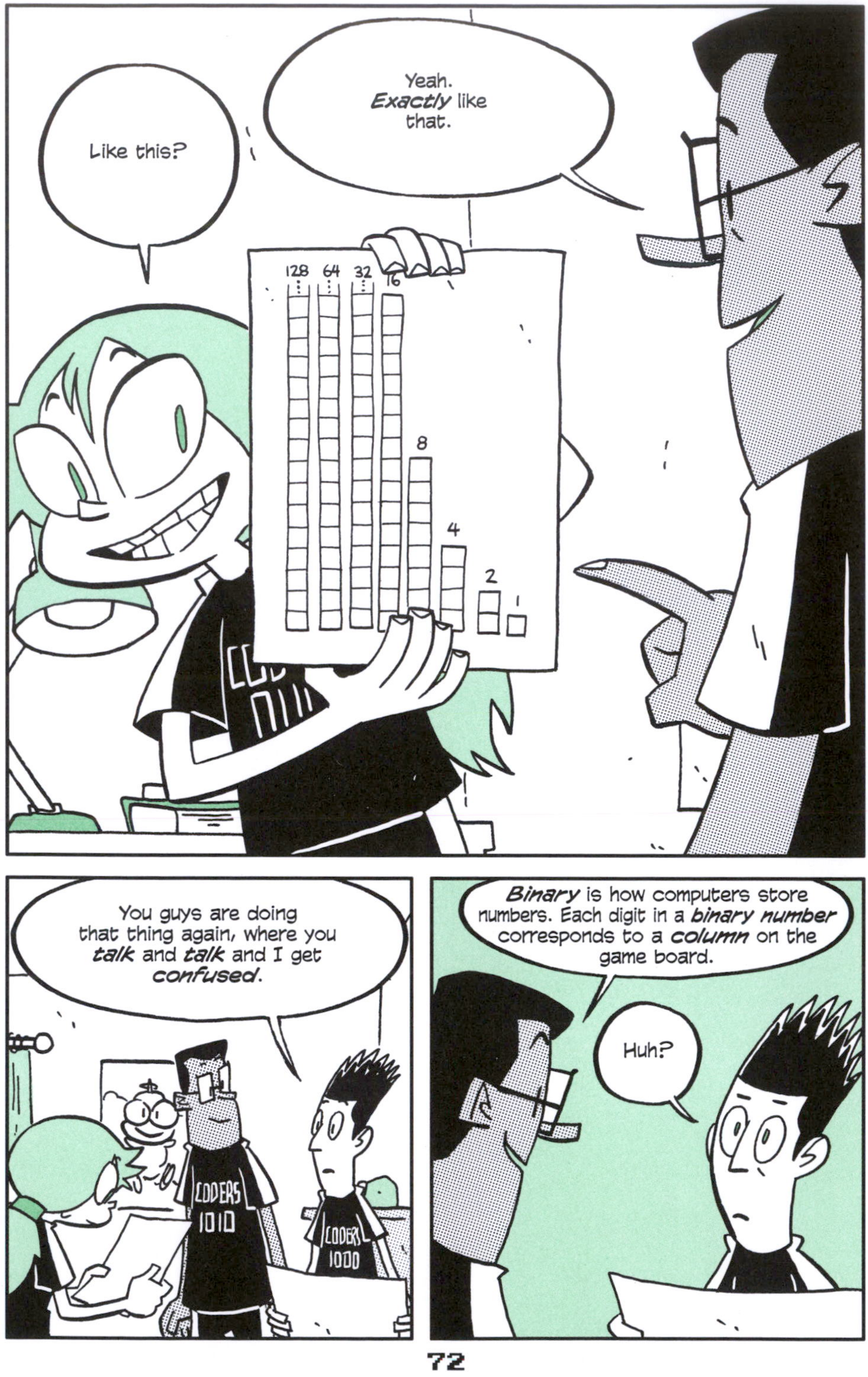
Like this?
Yeah. *Exactly* like that.
128
64
32
16
8
4
2
1
You guys are doing that thing again, where you *talk* and *talk* and I get *confused*.
CODERS 1010
CODERS 1000
Binary is how computers store numbers. Each digit in a *binary number* corresponds to a *column* on the game board.
Huh?

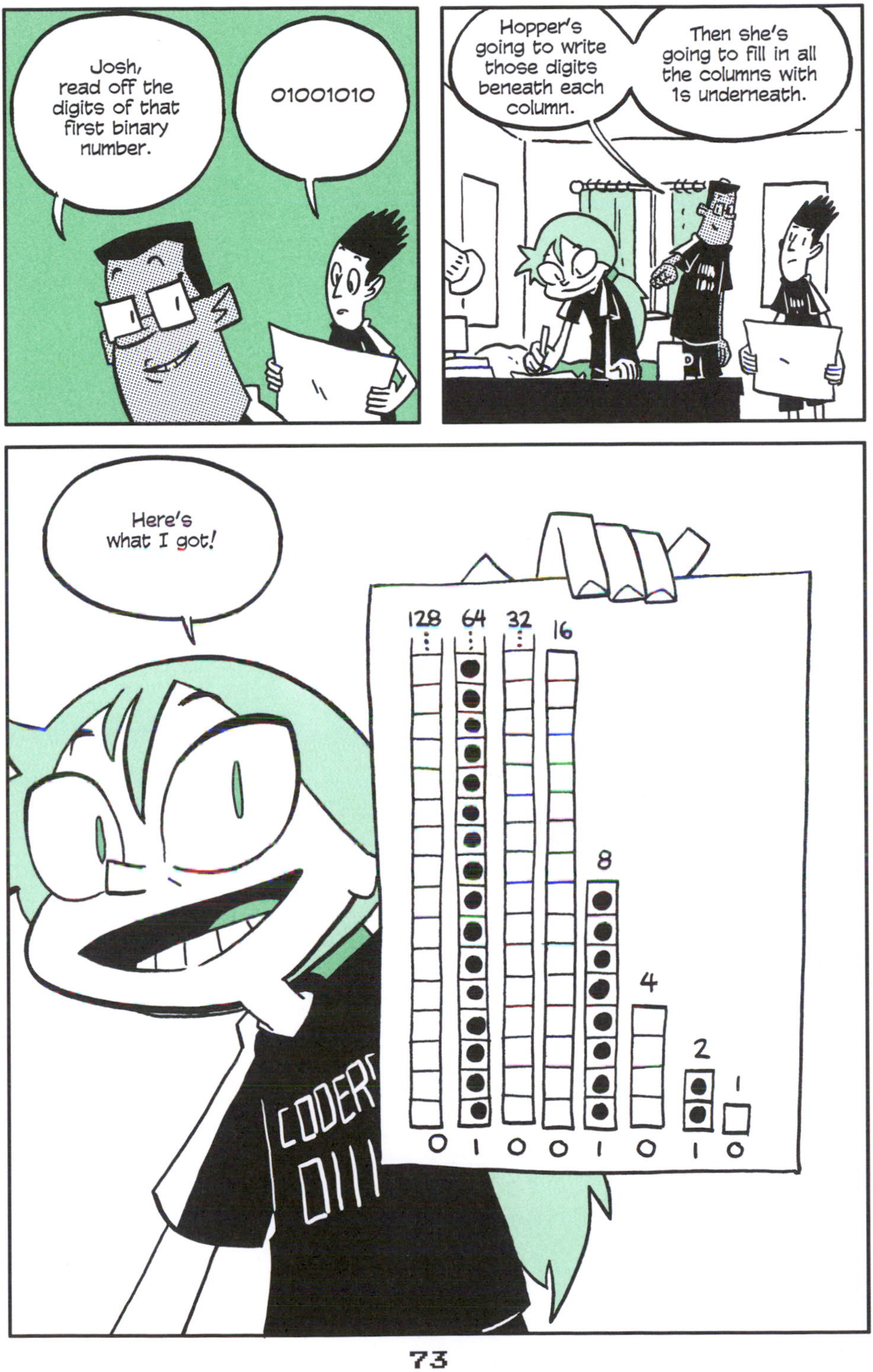
Josh, read off the digits of that first binary number.
01001010
Hopper's going to write those digits beneath each column.
Then she's going to fill in all the columns with 1s underneath.
Here's what I got!
128
64
32
16
8
4
2
1
0 1 0 0 1 0 1 0
CODERS
0111

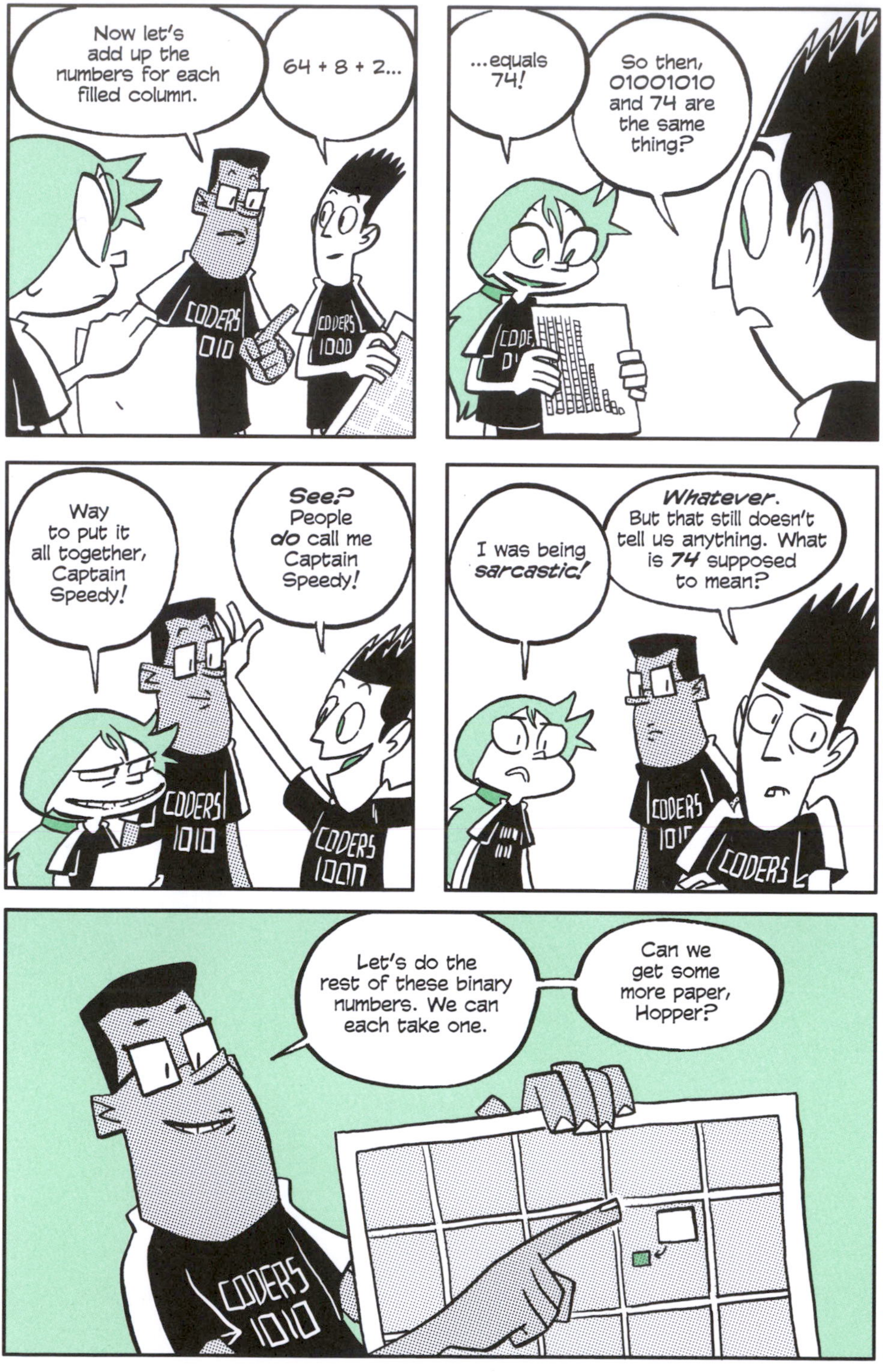
Now let's add up the numbers for each filled column.
64 + 8 + 2...
CODERS 1010
CODERS 1000
...equals 74!
So then, 01001010 and 74 are the same thing?
Way to put it all together, Captain Speedy!
See? People do call me Captain Speedy!
CODERS 1010
CODERS 1000
I was being sarcastic!
Whatever. But that still doesn't tell us anything. What is 74 supposed to mean?
CODERS
Let's do the rest of these binary numbers. We can each take one.
Can we get some more paper, Hopper?
CODERS 1010

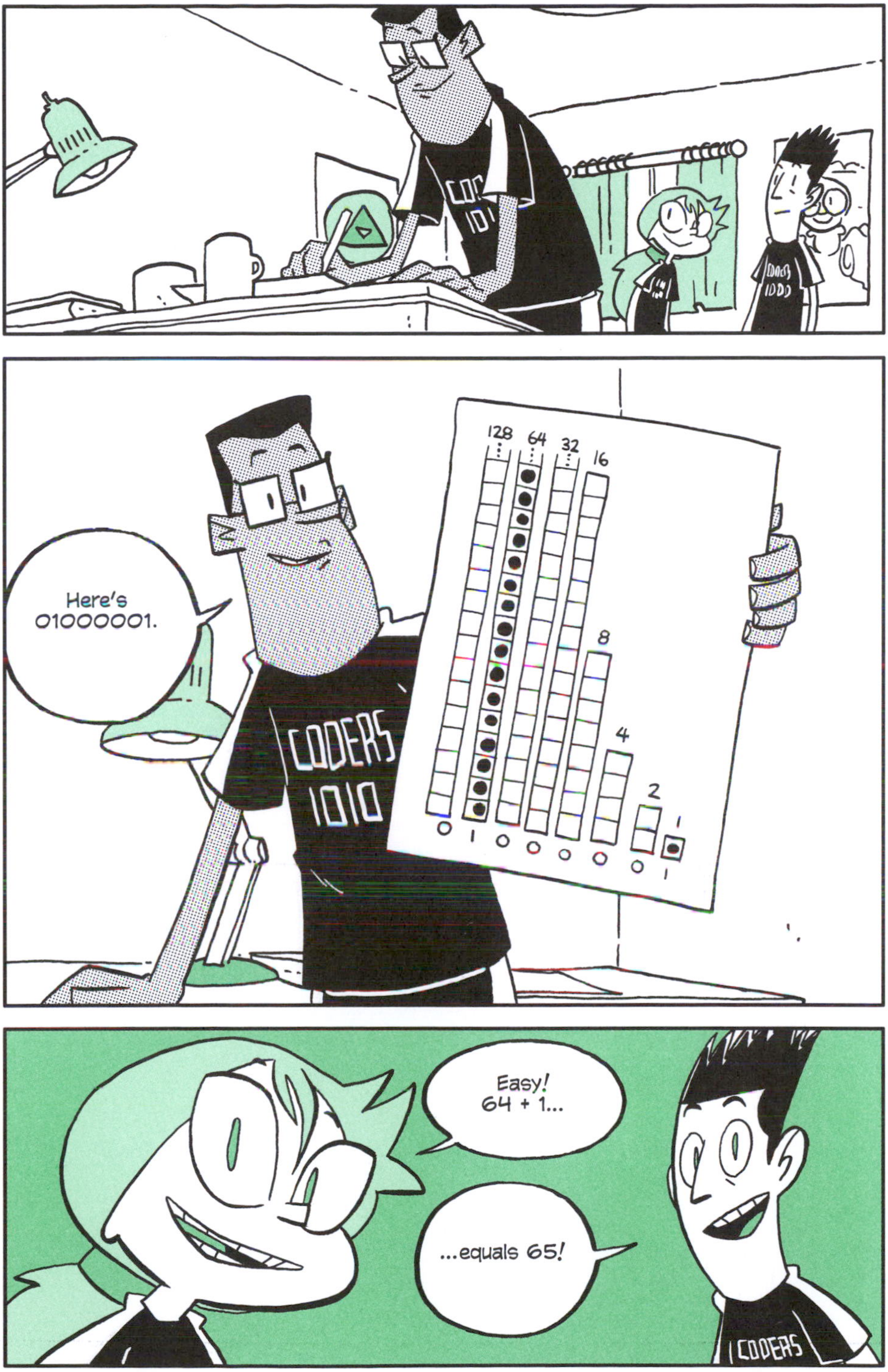
CODERS 1010
128
64
32
16
8
4
2
1
0 1 0 0 0 0 0 1
Here's 01000001.
Easy! 64 + 1...
...equals 65!
CODERS

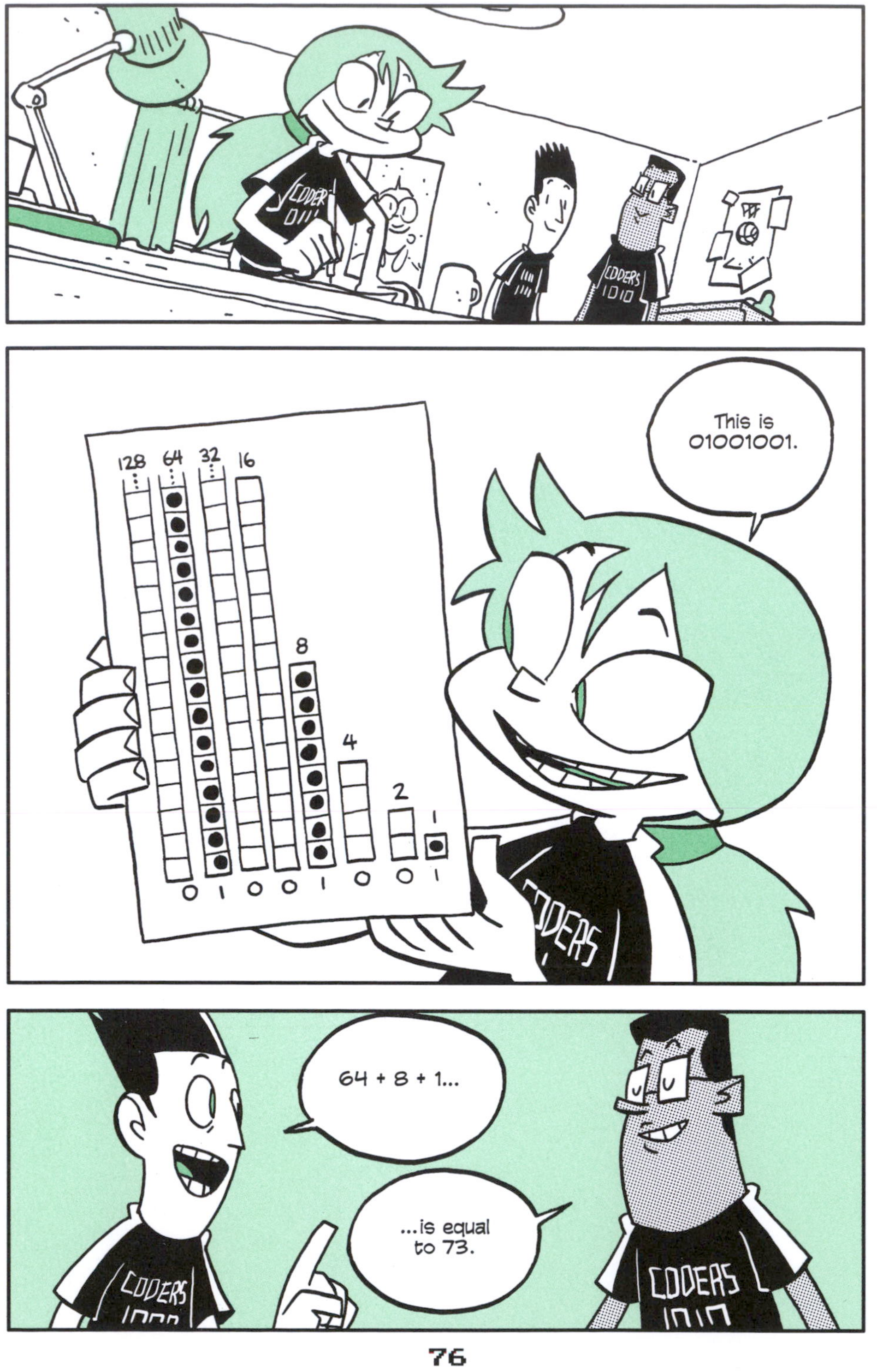
CODERS 1010
CODERS 1010
128
64
32
16
8
4
2
1
0 1 0 0 1 0 0 1
This is 01001001.
CODERS
64 + 8 + 1...
...is equal to 73.
CODERS
CODERS 1010

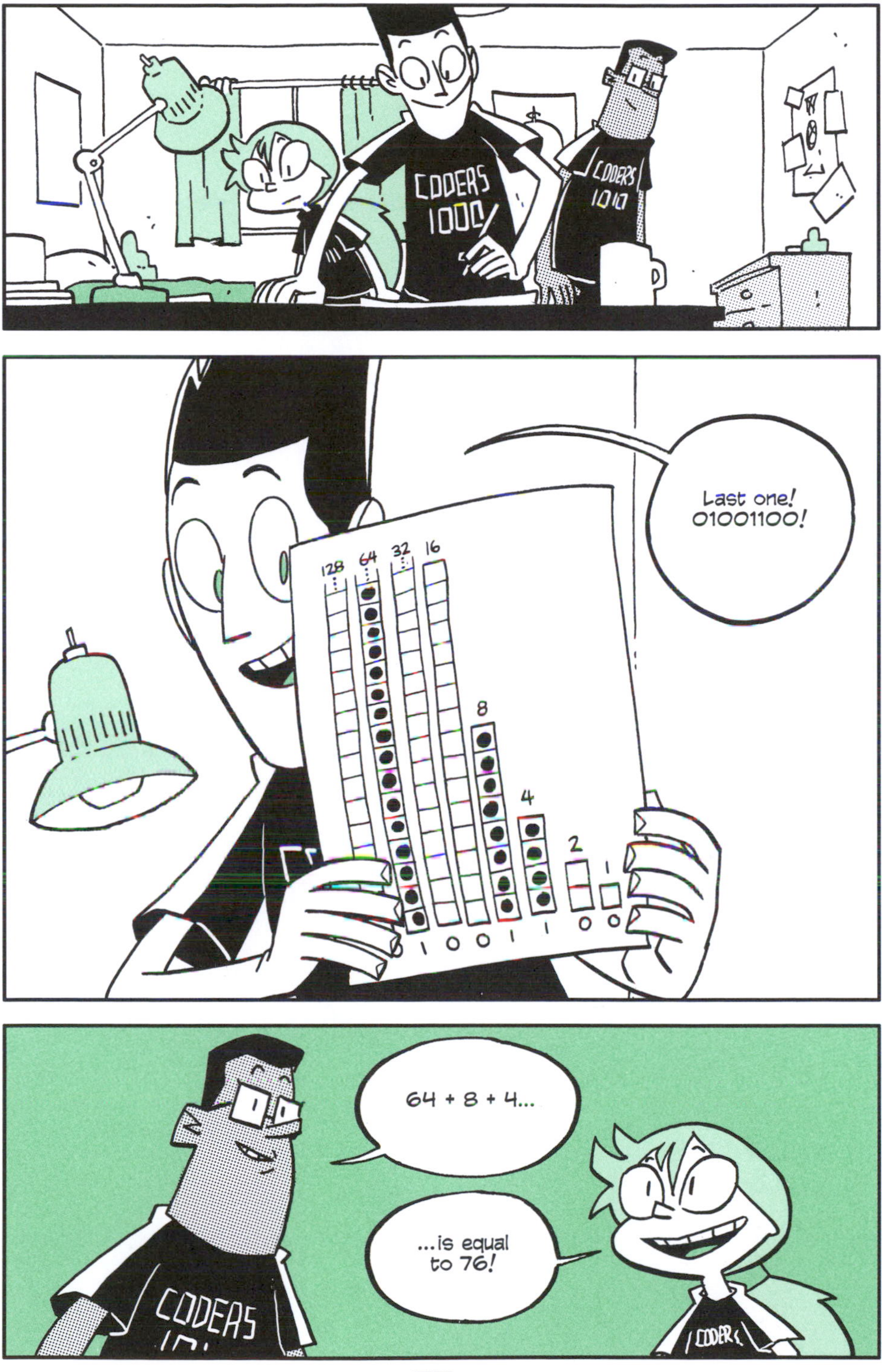
Last one!
01001100!
64 + 8 + 4...
...is equal
to 76!

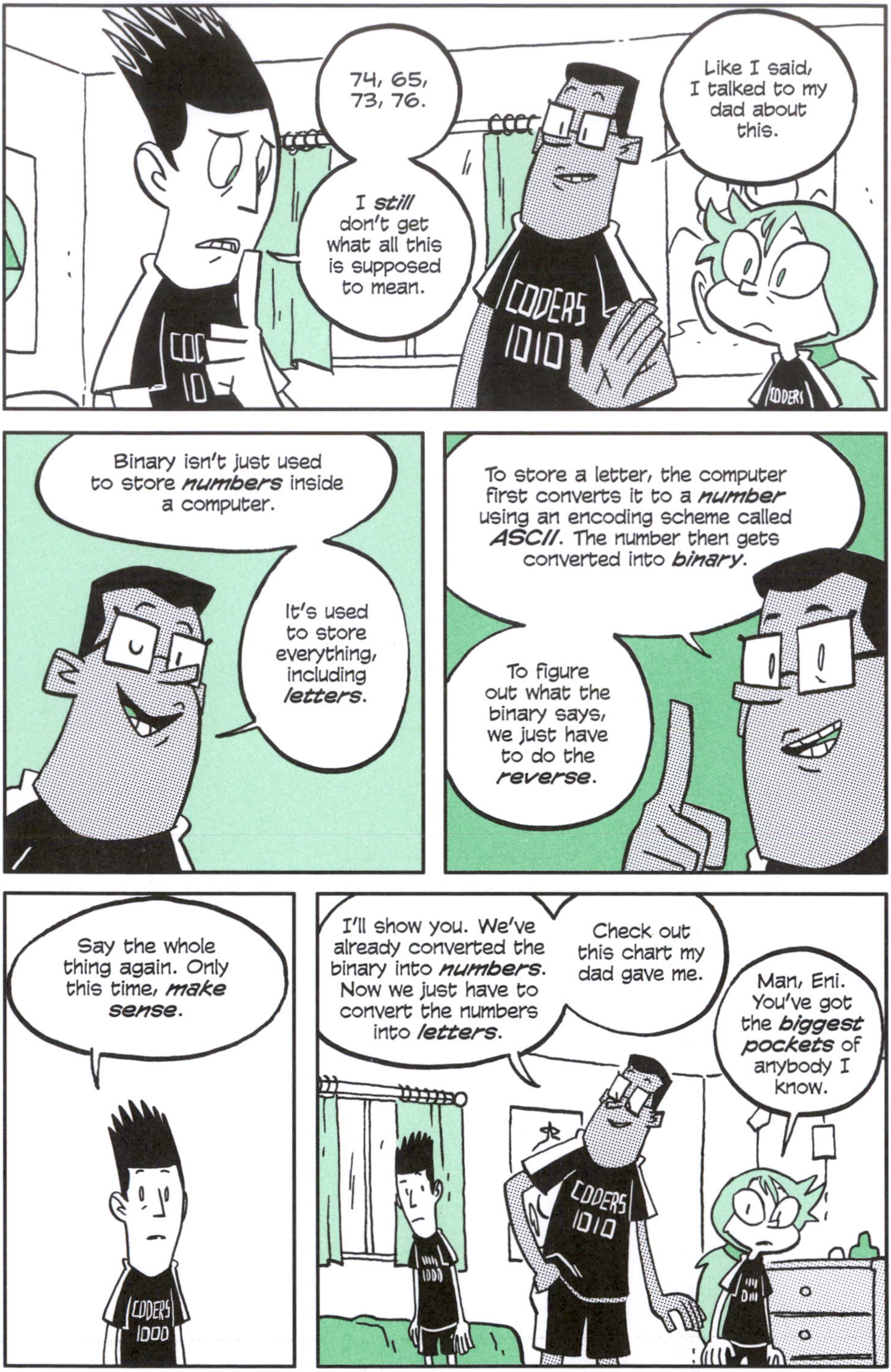
74, 65, 73, 76.
I *still* don't get what all this is supposed to mean.
Like I said, I talked to my dad about this.
CODERS 1010
Binary isn't just used to store *numbers* inside a computer.
It's used to store everything, including *letters*.
To store a letter, the computer first converts it to a *number* using an encoding scheme called *ASCII*. The number then gets converted into *binary*.
To figure out what the binary says, we just have to do the *reverse*.
Say the whole thing again. Only this time, *make sense*.
CODERS 1000
I'll show you. We've already converted the binary into *numbers*. Now we just have to convert the numbers into *letters*.
Check out this chart my dad gave me.
Man, Eni. You've got the *biggest pockets* of anybody I know.
CODERS 1010

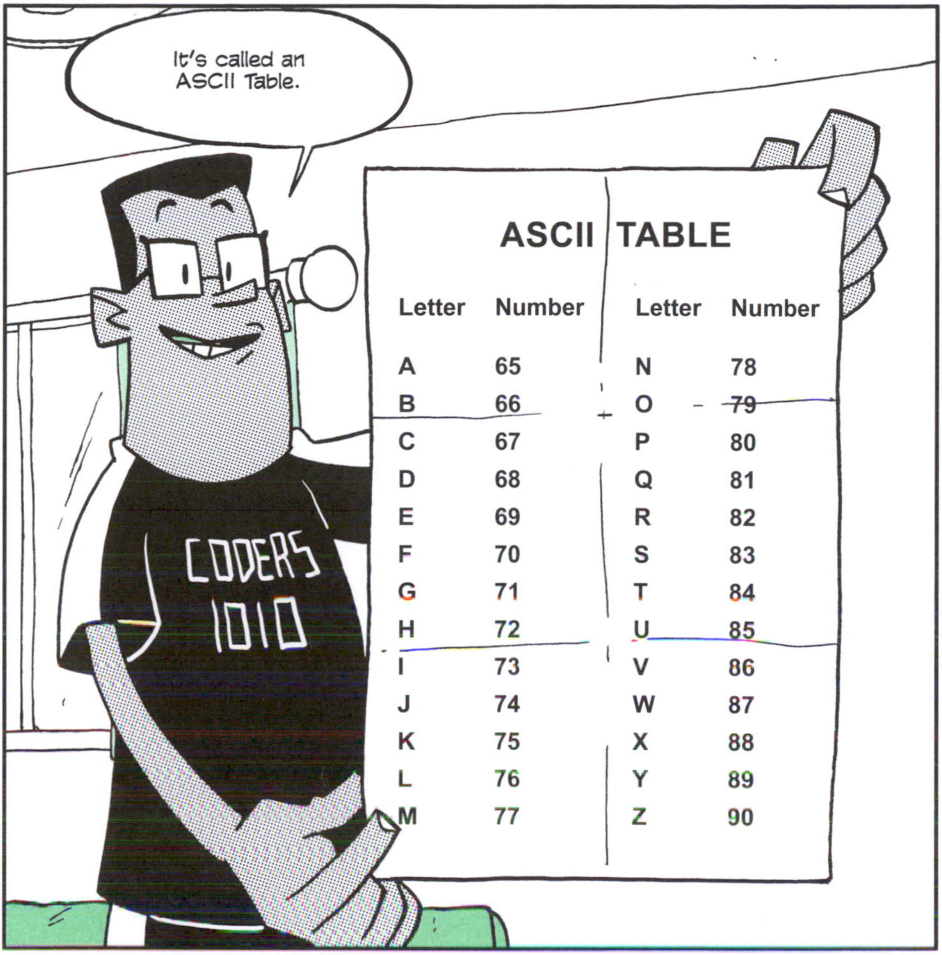
It's called an ASCII Table.
ASCII TABLE
Letter Number Letter Number
A 65 N 78
B 66 O 79
C 67 P 80
D 68 Q 81
E 69 R 82
F 70 S 83
G 71 T 84
H 72 U 85
I 73 V 86
J 74 W 87
K 75 X 88
L 76 Y 89
M 77 Z 90
CODERS 1010

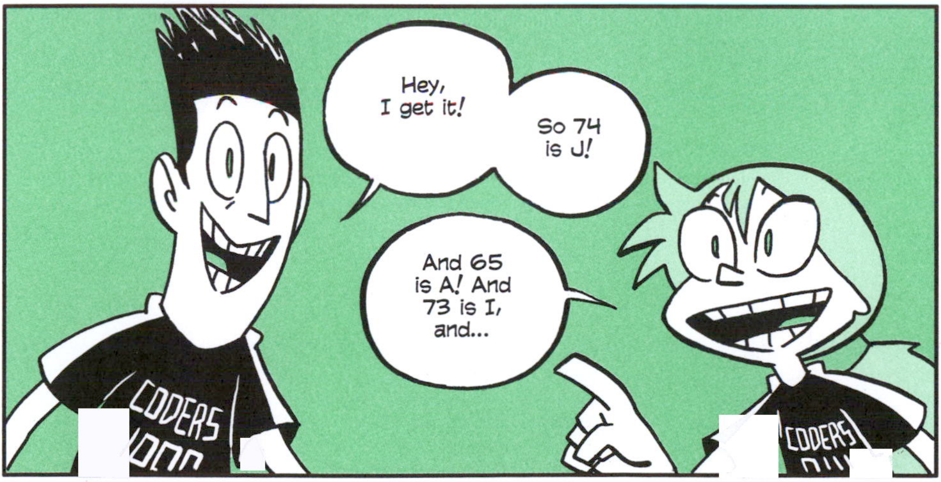
Hey, I get it!
So 74 is J!
And 65 is A! And 73 is I, and...

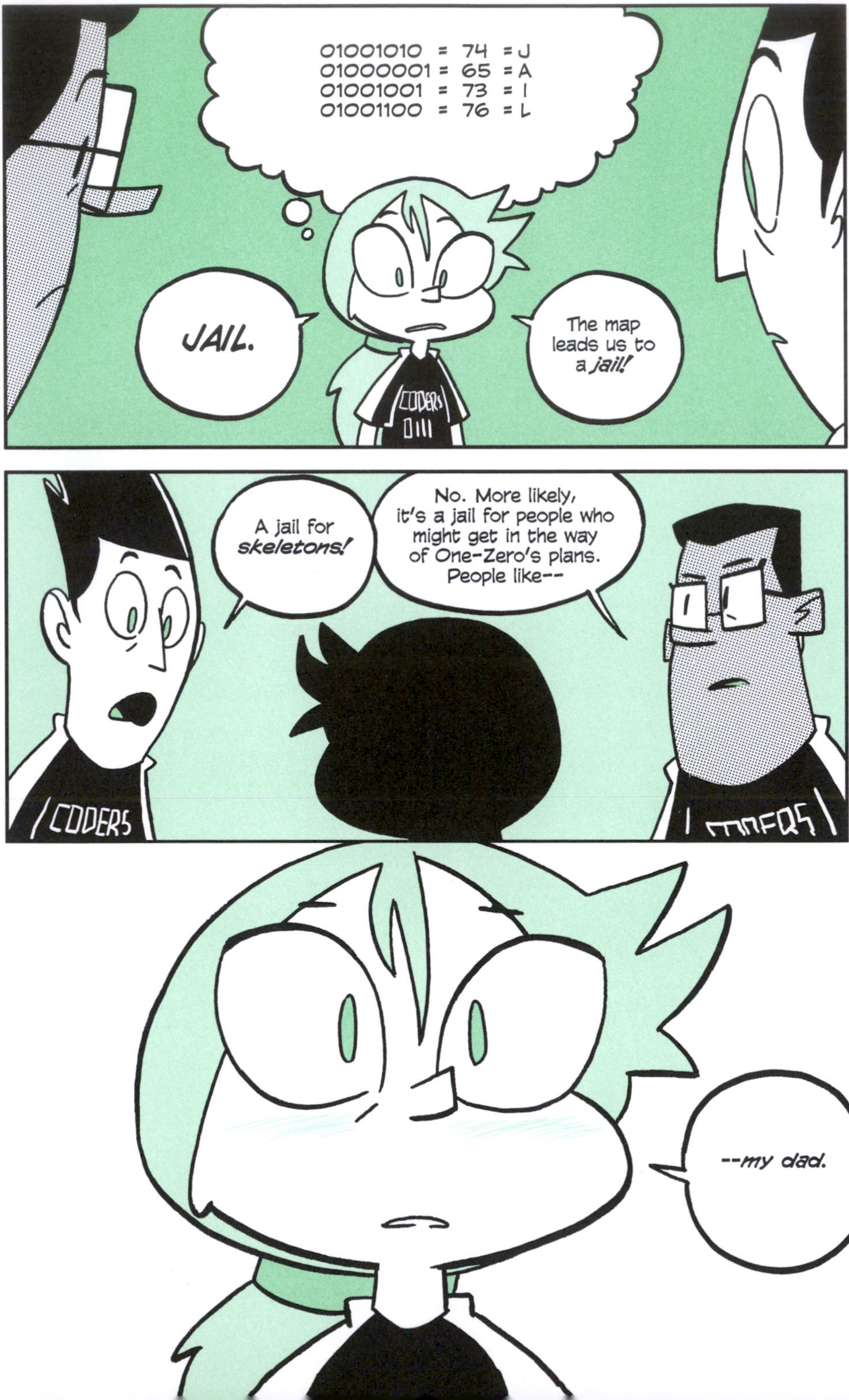
01001010 = 74 = J
01000001 = 65 = A
01001001 = 73 = I
01001100 = 76 = L
JAIL.
The map leads us to a *jail!*
CODERS
A jail for *skeletons!*
No. More likely, it's a jail for people who might get in the way of One-Zero's plans. People like--
CODERS
--my dad.

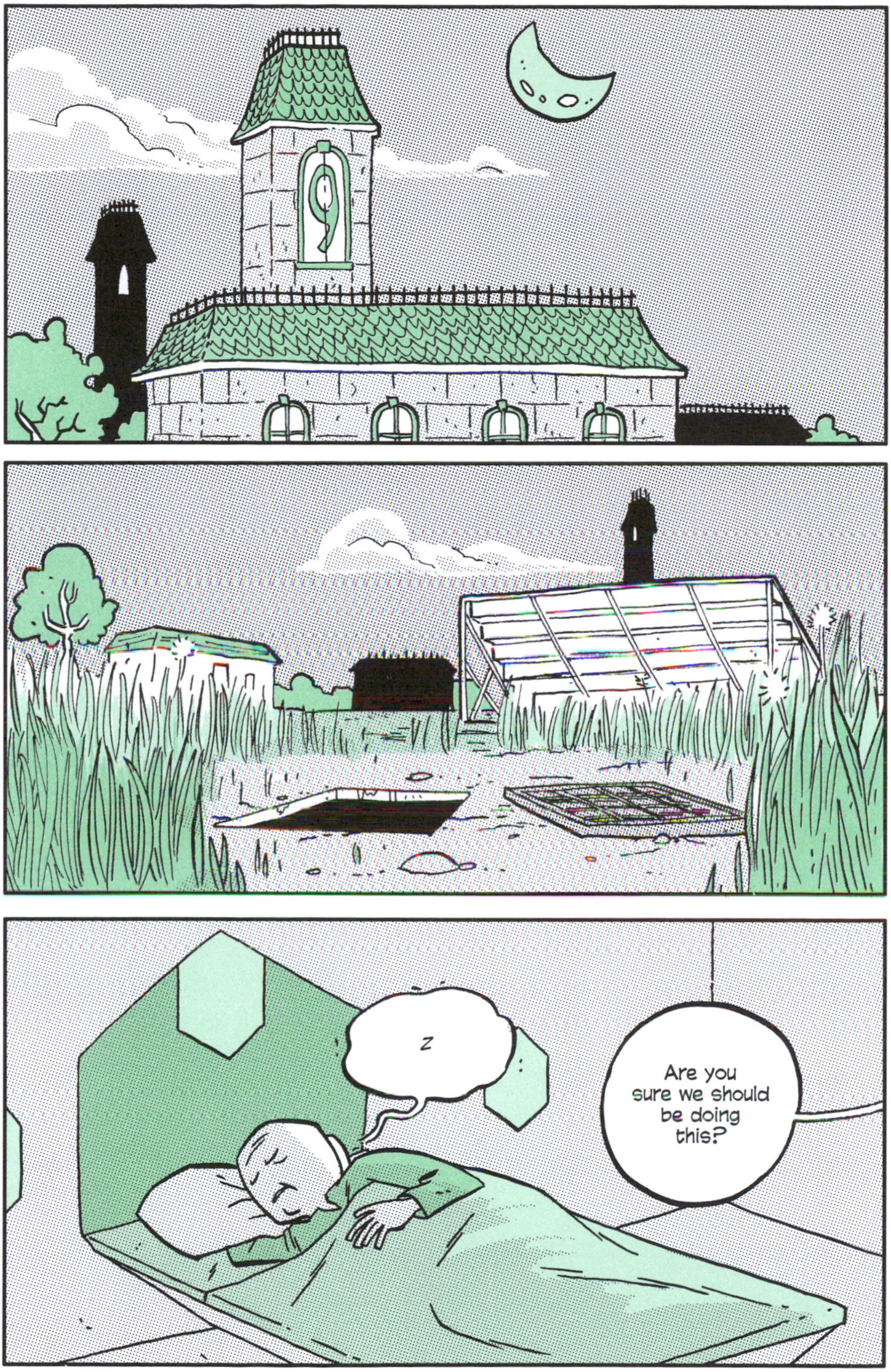
z
Are you sure we should be doing this?

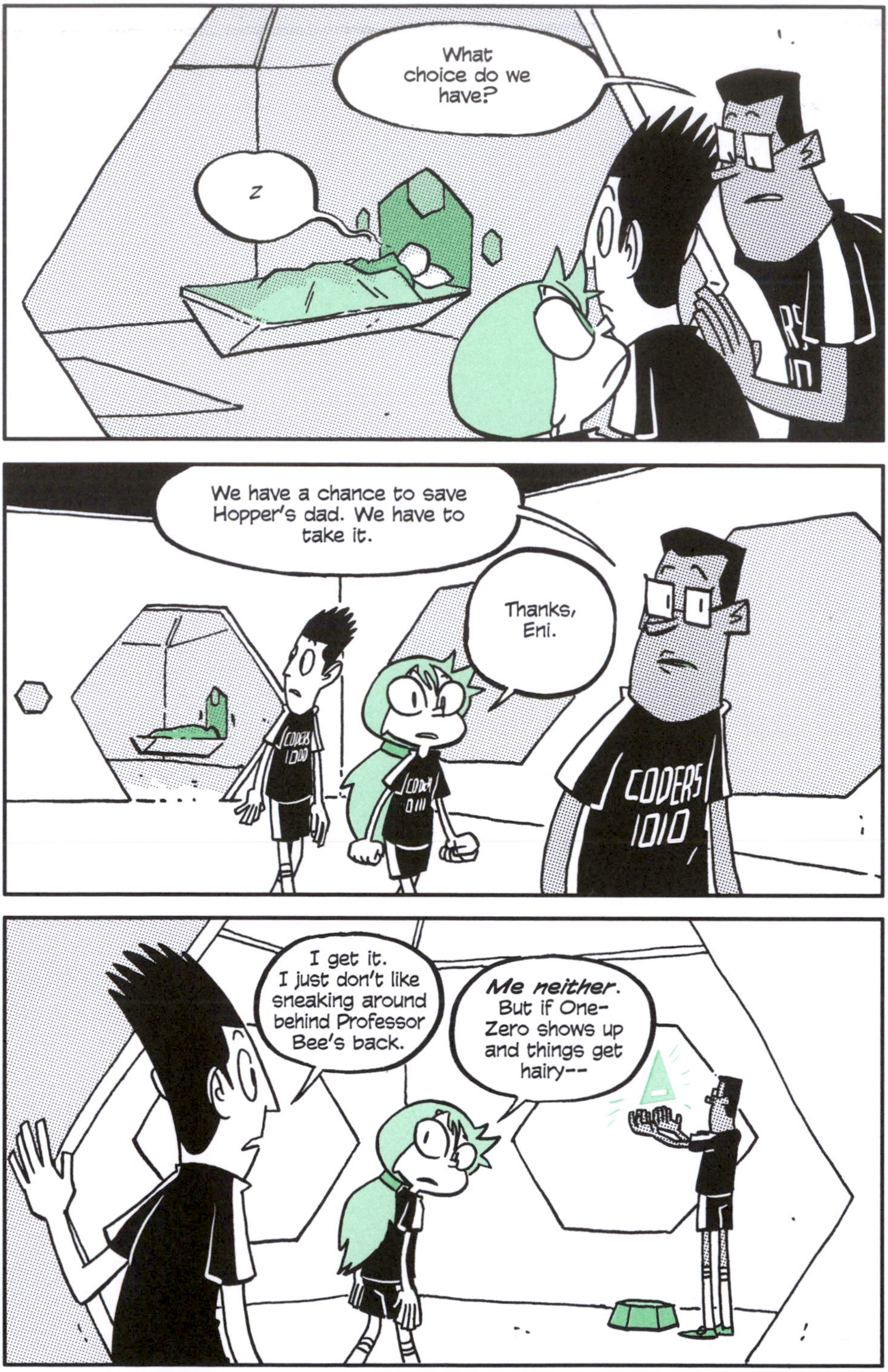
What choice do we have?
Z
We have a chance to save Hopper's dad. We have to take it.
Thanks, Eni.
I get it. I just don't like sneaking around behind Professor Bee's back.
Me neither. But if One-Zero shows up and things get hairy--

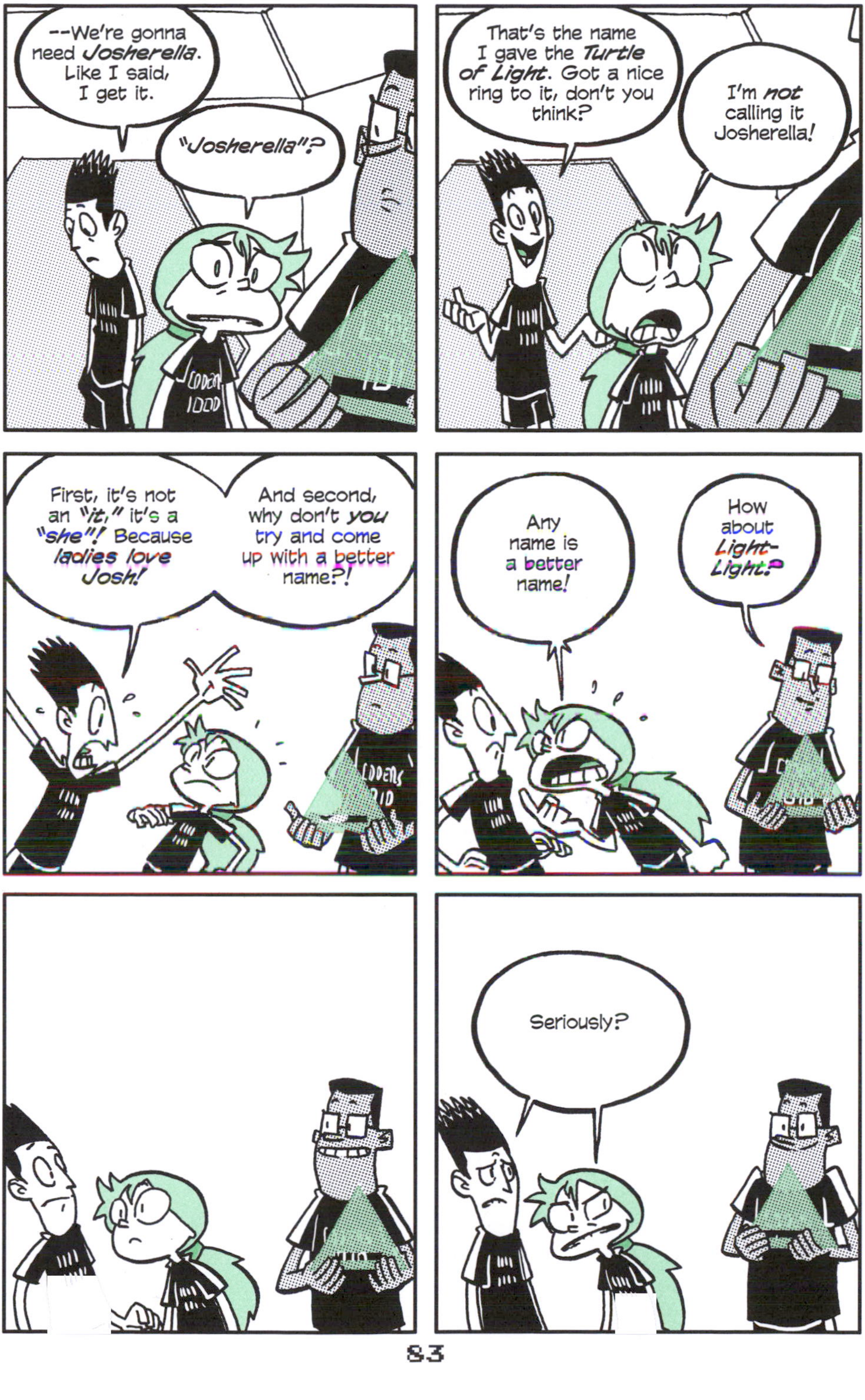
--We're gonna need Josherella. Like I said, I get it.
"Josherella"?
That's the name I gave the Turtle of Light. Got a nice ring to it, don't you think?
I'm not calling it Josherella!
First, it's not an "it," it's a "she"! Because ladies love Josh!
And second, why don't you try and come up with a better name?!
Any name is a better name!
How about Light-Light?
Seriously?

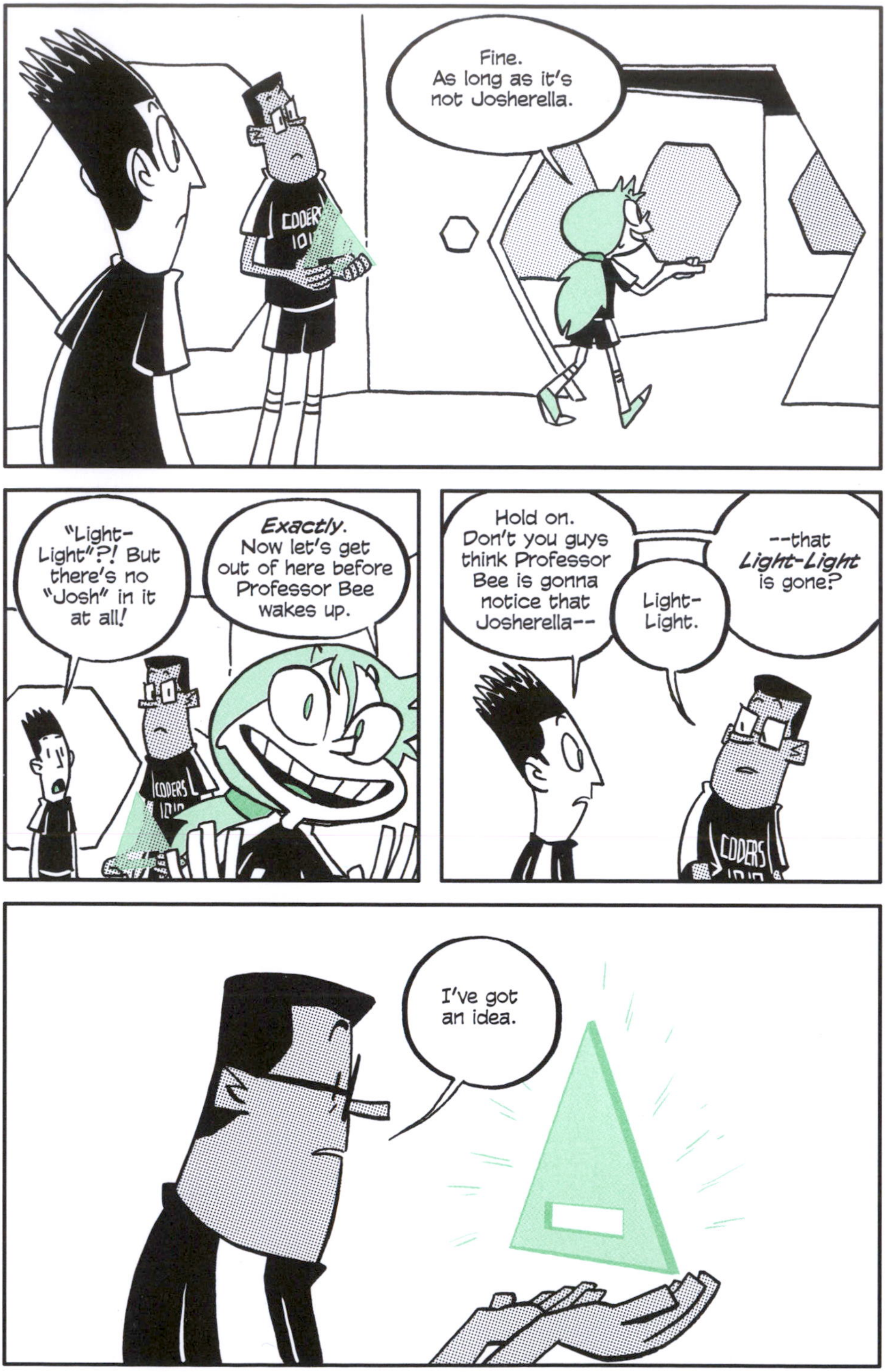
Fine.
As long as it's not Josherella.
"Light-Light"?! But there's no "Josh" in it at all!
Exactly. Now let's get out of here before Professor Bee wakes up.
Hold on. Don't you guys think Professor Bee is gonna notice that Josherella--
Light-Light.
--that *Light-Light* is gone?
I've got an idea.

```
Left 90
Repeat 3 [
    Forward 10
    Right 120
]
Forward 2
Right 90
Forward 2
Left 90
Forward 6
Left 90
Forward 2
```

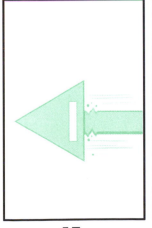

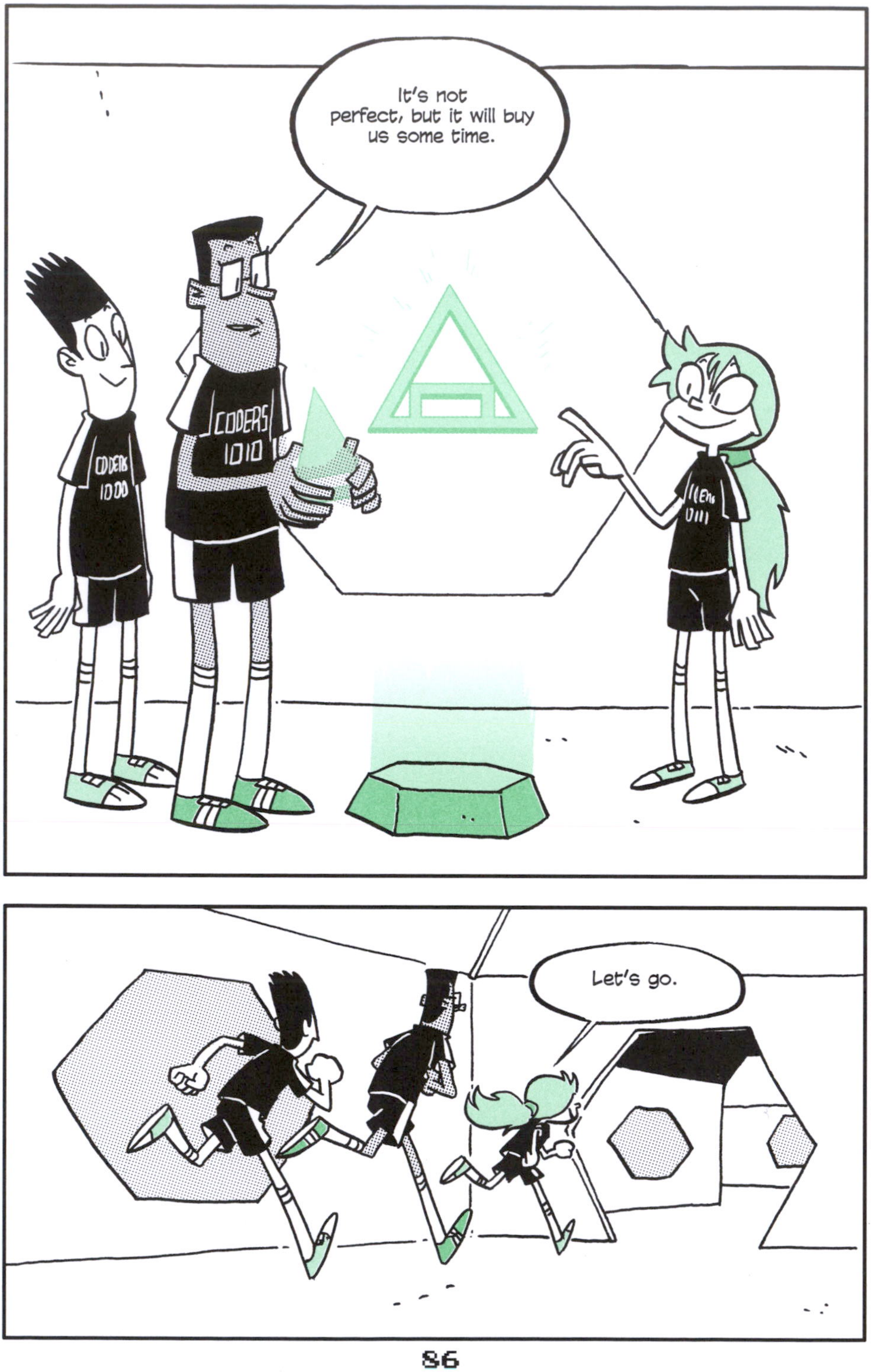
It's not perfect, but it will buy us some time.
CODERS 1010
Let's go.

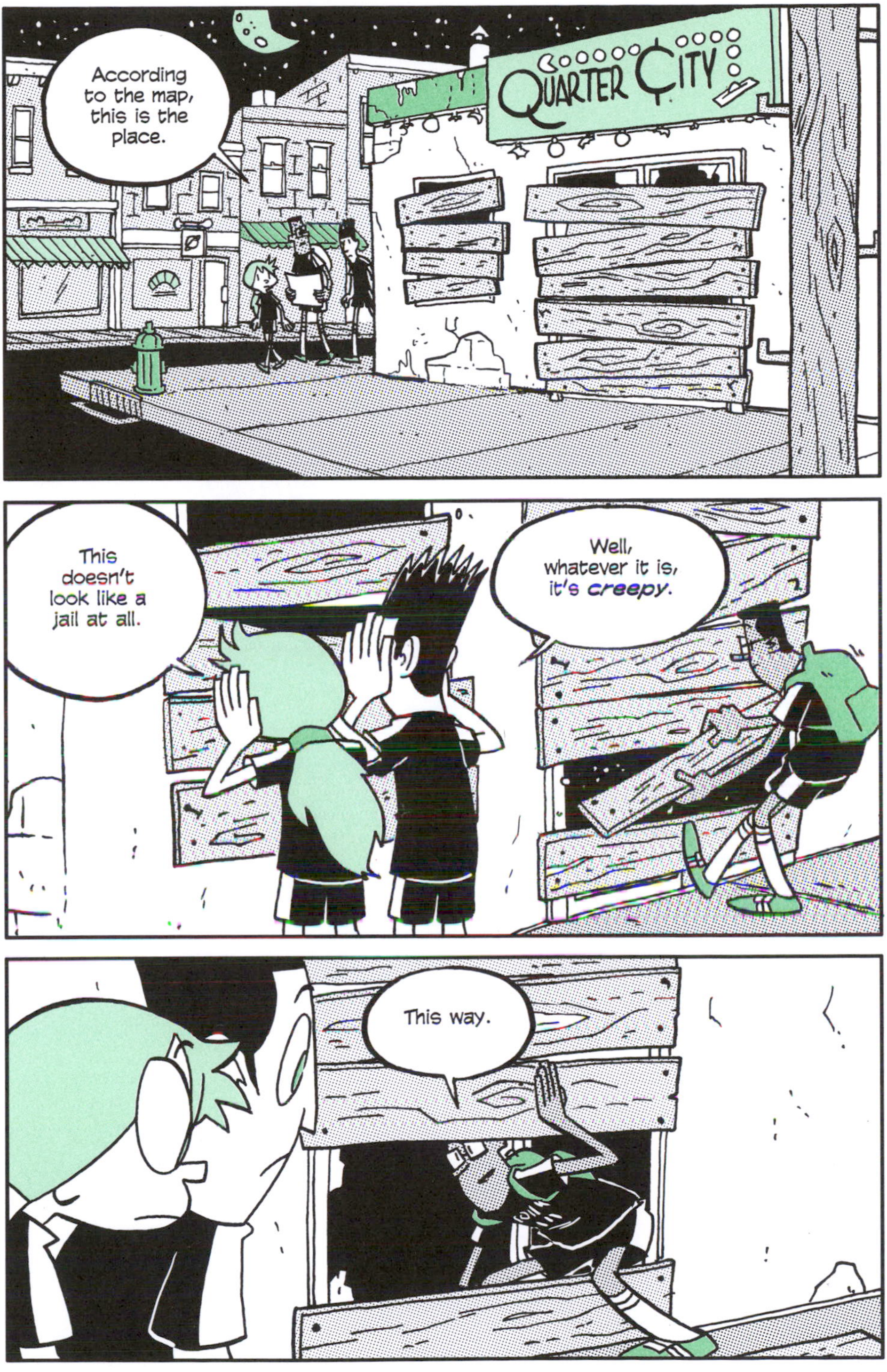
QUARTER CITY
According to the map, this is the place.
This doesn't look like a jail at all.
Well, whatever it is, it's *creepy*.
This way.

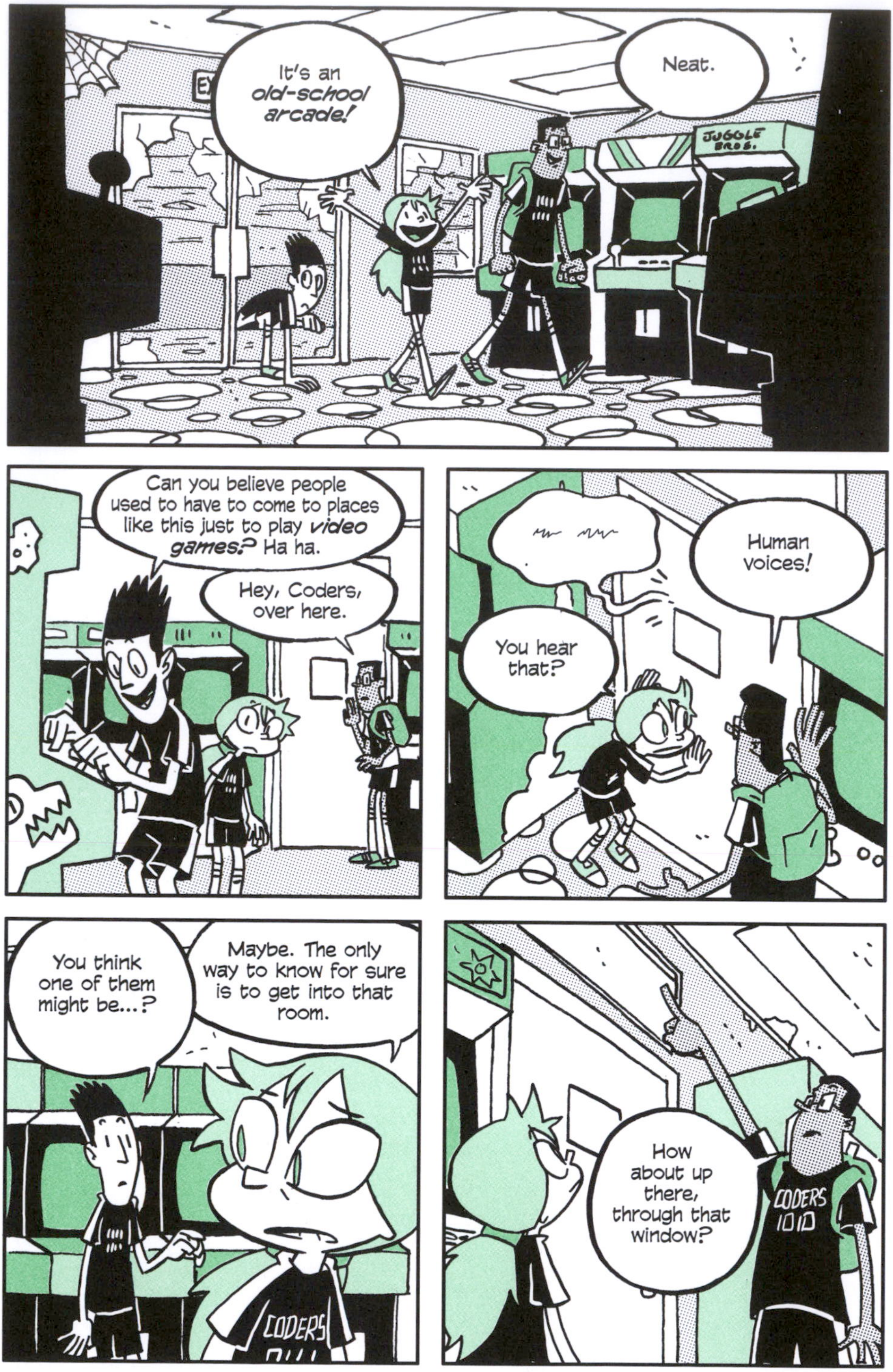
It's an *old-school arcade!*
Neat.
JUGGLE BROS.
Can you believe people used to have to come to places like this just to play *video games?* Ha ha.
Hey, Coders, over here.
You hear that?
Human voices!
You think one of them might be...?
Maybe. The only way to know for sure is to get into that room.
How about up there, through that window?
CODERS 1010

! QUACK

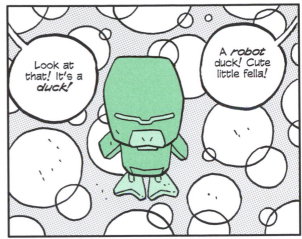

Look at that! It's a *duck!*

A *robot* duck! Cute little fella!

Careful. *One-Zero* probably built that duck.

Oh, come on! How dangerous could it be? It's a *duck!*

Yeow!

SNAP

Ducks aren't supposed to have *teeth!* That's *cheating!*

Up here!

Oh no.

QUACK QUACK

89

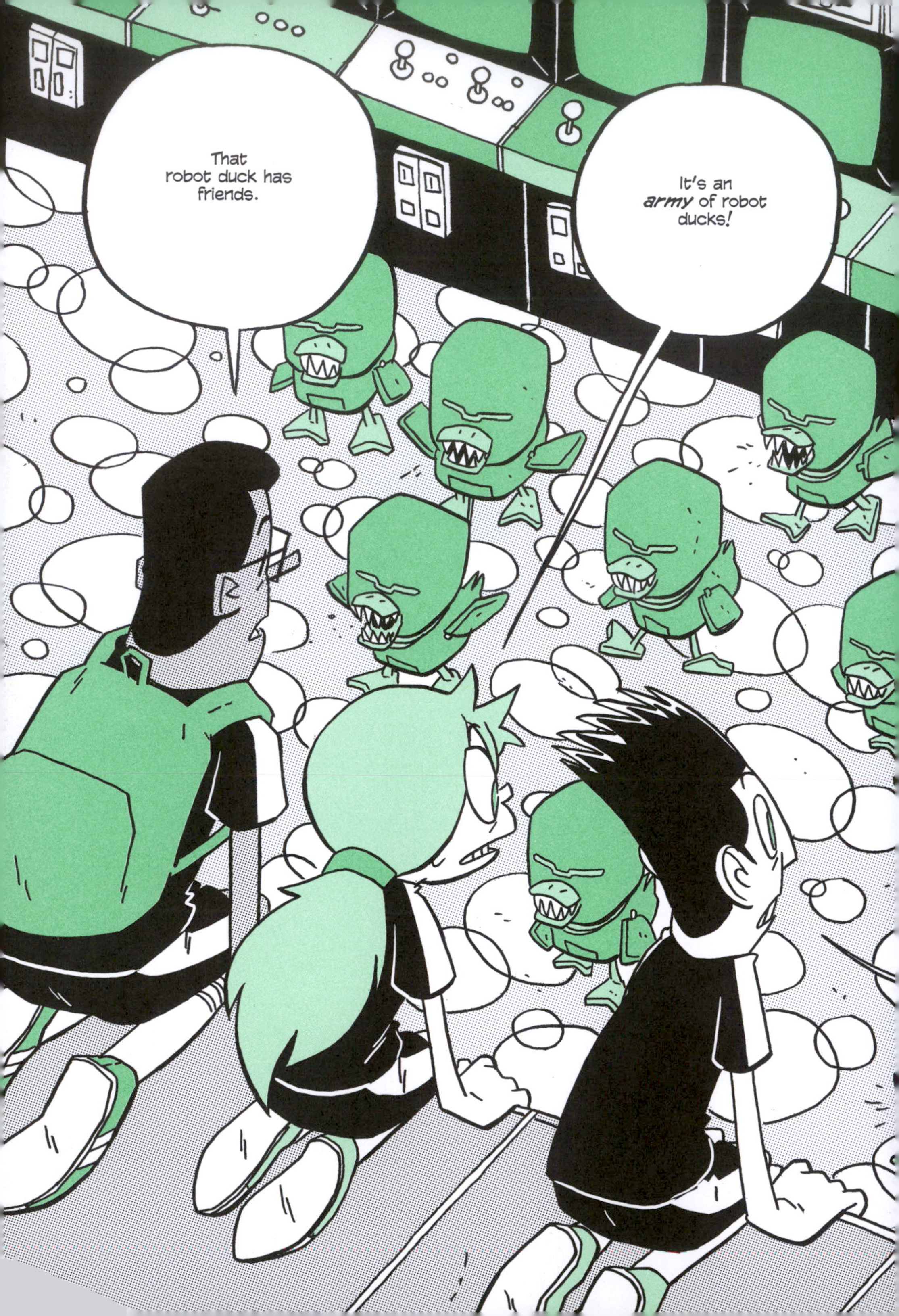
That robot duck has friends.
It's an *army* of robot ducks!

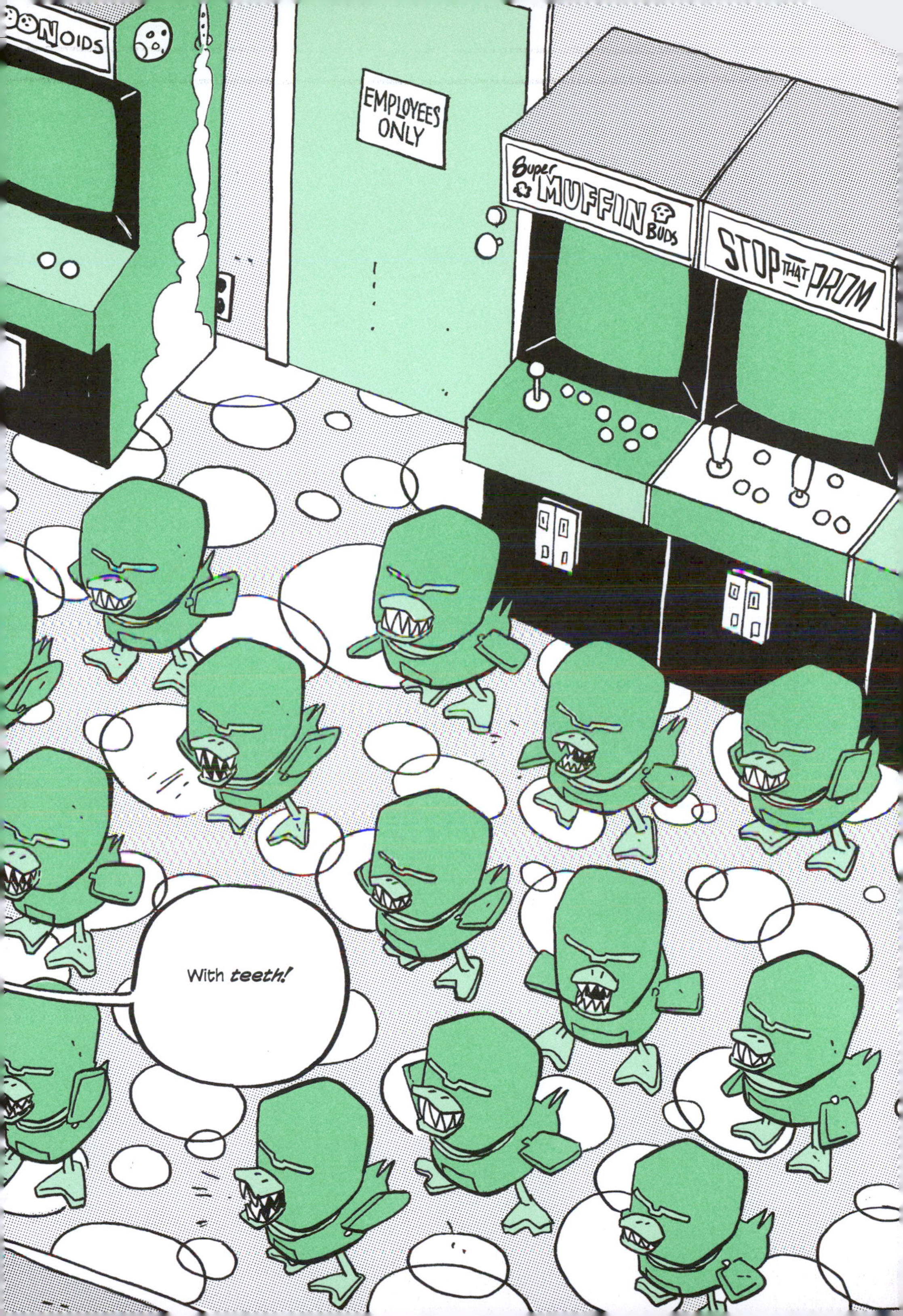

EMPLOYEES ONLY
Super MUFFIN BUDS
STOP THAT PROM
With *teeth!*

Ducks with teeth are so *not cute*.

We have to get to the other side!

Time for *Light-Light*.

Good thinking! How many steps do you think it'll take to get all the way across? One hundred, maybe?

About that.

We can make a bridge that's sort of like a *ladder*, only it goes across instead of up.

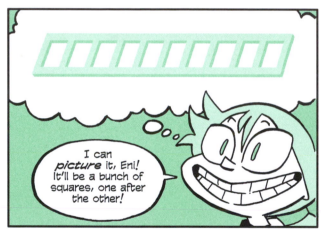

I can *picture* it, Eni! It'll be a bunch of squares, one after the other!

We can use *nested Repeats*.

Josh! Bringing your A game!

Okay, we're gonna pause once more.

Let's do this, Coders!

Can you come up with code that makes a ladder-like bridge out of squares?